D1525743

Shriek

By Jeffrey B Miley

Copyright 2018

Table of Contents

Chapter One

Trail Cam

The weather was beginning to change and soon the leaves would follow suit. Cain loved the fall. The brisk air tinged with the smell of wood smoke from someone's chimney or fire pit was the harbinger that signaled summer was finally at an end.

He was also eager to say goodbye to the mosquitoes and gnats that have always plagued his working life. There was always a downside to any job. Unfortunately, Cain could name a few more unpleasant aspects of being a Fish and Game officer, chief of which were the morons who hunted out of season or ignored the legal limits of the hunting and fishing seasons.

After nineteen years of policing the great outdoors, he had begun to appreciate his last promotion. Becoming Resident Agent In Charge, or RAC, of the Western Pennsylvania Region required that he spend more time behind a desk. It was a good assignment to receive as his thoughts turned to retirement, for which he was eligible in about six years. After twenty-five years his pension would be very attractive. *What could go wrong?* he thought.

He was about to find out.

Cain looked up from his desk as a visitor walked in dressed in more flannel than what could be considered in good taste. It was Deacon Humboldt, self-proclaimed wildlife expert and local Grizzly Adams look-like. The major qualifications for the last being that he never shaved and only took a shower about once a month. For reference, the local Amish found his personal hygiene disgusting.

Cain and Deke had been friends for years. Not withstanding his smell, Deke was a good man. He was honest, faithful and the funniest man that Cain had ever encountered. He was always welcome because he lightened the mood whenever he arrived.

Looking at his friend, Cain knew this was going to be a different type of encounter.

"What's wrong, Deke? You look agitated as hell."

"Yeah, but you could still say hello when you see a body walk in."

"Hello, Deke," Cain acquiesced.

"Don't hello me. I'm too upset for pleasantries."

Cain immediately barked out a laugh. This was classic Deke.

"Once more. What's wrong, Deke?" he repeated.

"I don't know where to start. Should I start with the ghost or the dead deer?"

The RAC didn't know how to react. As soon as he heard the word 'ghost' he began to wonder if Deke was about to string him along with an elaborate joke. The dead deer was what really caused Cain to doubt that there was humor involved. Deke was dead serious about his wildlife.

"Start with the ghost. That sounds intriguing to me."

"Okay. I'll start with my trail cam. Here, look," Deke said as he threw a series of black and white photos on Cain's desk. Cain picked them up. They were the typical monochrome images from an infrared trail camera. The primary image captured was a beautiful eight point buck with the white glowing eyes that were typical of such images. There was an additional point of interest to the far right in the photo.

"What do you think, Cain? Interesting, ain't it?"

Cain didn't answer. He looked more closely at the image on the right. There was no point looking any further at the deer. It was very clear, but the other image looked as if it was glowing.

"C'mon, Cain. What does that look like to you?"

Cain refused to be rushed. Yes, Deke was a good man, but he loved drama. He liked to gossip and spin yarns. Cain didn't want to start anything. He wanted to examine the photo a moment longer and then choose his words carefully.

"Dammit ranger, tell me what you see. In plain English so I don't misconstrue anything. You know how I like to be dead nuts accurate about these things."

"Well first, stop calling me ranger. I am an officer or a warden. And second, I see what appears to be a woman dressed in a light colored garment standing off to the side behind the deer. It is a little indistinct, but she appears to be screaming towards the deer, or maybe the camera."

"That's the ghost, Penelope Sutter. She was a bride and on her wedding day, right before the 'I do's' she was accused by two women of being a witch. Right there in the church during the ceremony. People got a might upset. The story goes that a self-appointed vigilante group grabbed her and dragged her into the woods. When the group came back out of the woods, Penelope wasn't with them. No one ever saw her again. How do you like them apples, Cain?"

"Cute story, Deke. When did this supposedly happen?"

"1817. And right here in Canoe Creek. The forest was a lot bigger back then. I believe it was in September, after the harvest. That's when they did weddings and such. Always after the harvest, once the work was done. I read all this in a book called, The History of Blair County. That's a picture of the real Blair witch, not that made up crap from Hollywood."

"Why couldn't this just be a woman out for a walk?"

"Damn, Cain. You're a cop…of sorts. Don't you see the timestamp? Three ought five in the lower left corner. Nobody goes walking in the woods at 3:05 *a.m.* Nobody."

"People are strange. What else has you convinced this is a witch or a ghost or whatever?"

"The deer, Cain. The damn deer. Let me show you Exhibit B."

Cain had to stifle a chuckle. Deke had obviously watched too many episodes of Perry Mason, Matlock, LA Law or any of the recent cheesy lawyer shows. If Deke kept acting like a backwoods lawyer, Cain was going to lose it.

"When I go out in the woods, I am always prepared. I bring my sixteen megapixel Kodak digital camera. And before you say something smart ass, yes, I am a renaissance man. I use computers and everything. Now slip this smart card into your laptop and have a look."

Cain complied with his friend's request. Within two minutes he found himself looking at an animal carcass. He saw a deer's head lying a few feet away from the main trunk, which appeared to be missing its legs.

A few photos later he was staring at the legs. At first he wasn't sure they were legs because each one had long strands of flesh and fur hanging loosely around them. The carnage was horrendous.

"Holy shit, Deke. Why would somebody do this?"

"It wasn't a regular somebody, Ranger. It was a pissed off ghost."

"Why would a ghost butcher a deer out in the woods? And quit calling me *Ranger!*"

"That deer wasn't butchered, Cain. It was torn apart. I butcher deer for myself and my friends, and I'm telling you there ain't one blade mark on that deer. Not a pocket knife, a butcher knife, a saw, a machete or hatchet. That poor creature was rend apart limb from limb. And going by the blood spatter, it was alive while it was happening."

Cain locked up the office and followed Deke. He needed to see this for himself.

Chapter Two

Hikers Everywhere

Warden Jeremy Cain had never seen anything like the carnage he saw with Deke. In his nineteen year career he had seen victims, both human and animal, of bear and mountain lion attacks. But nothing that he could recall compared to what he had just seen.

He had taken his own camera, which was an old six pixel point and shoot that the state owned. But he didn't take any pictures of his own. He already had Deke's photos on his laptop. They were way better than anything he would have captured. And he needed the extreme detail to make the case that the deer had not been butchered by a man.

Of course, it was his job to think about what might have caused the deer's death. Men were not strong enough to do that. There were no ligature marks present, so mechanical means were eliminated. That leaves only one logical conclusion. It was a beast of some kind. The thought made him shiver. There were no claw marks or discernible bite wounds. Whatever did this grabbed the deer and simply separated the head and legs from the body. *What in the hell could do that?* he wondered.

More than thirty-five miles away in Rothrock State Park, four hikers and a dog were getting ready to pick a spot to put up their tents and settle in for the evening. Ken and his girlfriend Linda were the couple who instigated the outdoor foray and Ray and his wife Juanita were the willing companions. All four had been friends since college. The dog was named Biscuits and he belonged to Ray and Juanita. Maybe more correctly, they belonged to him.

No one in the group was particularly gifted as an outdoorsman, but that is the beauty of camping. You learn by your mistakes. They were impulsive and full of life. One of them said, "let's go hiking and camping," and the others said, "why not?"

There was still forty to fifty minutes of daylight left. The foursome found a clearing and began to pitch their tents. Each couple had invested in a nice two person hiker's tent. They were easy to set up and extremely lightweight. The night's accommodations were quickly set up with daylight to spare. The remaining time would be used to gather wood and tinder for a fire.

The men gathered the wood while the ladies found some rocks to make the fire circle. All were anticipating the next thing on their agenda which was to make an edible meal. Not one person in their little foursome was confident that the goal was achievable, but they were going to give it the old college try.

Their meal packs were freeze dried beef stroganoff with additional packs of red beans and rice. Although the meal pairing was not traditional, they were famished and looked forward to eating anything besides the salty beef jerky they had eaten on the trail.

While the humans went about their work, Biscuits occupied himself with sniffing the urine and scat that the local wildlife had left behind. There was more than enough to keep the canine happily sniffing for hours.

A fire was started with the aid of a Zippo lighter. Ken poured the contents of his canteen into a one quart stowaway pan from his backpack. Once the water was heated it would be poured directly into the freeze dried pouches of food. They couldn't wait.

They sat around their little campfire and reminisced about their old college days, which were only six years behind them. They laughed and argued. The food was prepared and, with the exception of being a touch too salty, it was agreed that it was extremely edible. Ray thought it was delicious, which began a round of making fun of Juanita's cooking. Juanita was not amused.

Biscuits was given some kibble that Juanita had stored in her backpack. The group's tummies were full. All was right with the world.

As the night cooled and the fire was stoked into a mighty blaze, Ken suggested that the group share ghost stories from their childhoods. Both women were less than enthusiastic, but Ray and Ken thought it would be great fun.

Ken started with a story about a crazy farmer, whom he said was from the local area, of course, who lost his mind and killed his entire family with a pitchfork. The family was found slaughtered, but the farmer was never caught and brought to justice.

"It is said that he still roams these woods to this very day," Ken intoned and shouted,"BOO!"

The girls jumped and Juanita screamed that she thought she peed herself. They all laughed uncontrollably for a full three minutes.

"My turn, my turn," Ray said hurriedly.

They got quiet as Ray began.

"This is a true story. I read it in some ghost book from this area. It was pretty cool."

The fire crackled and popped.

"A woman named Penelope Sutter was getting married. I mean this happened right in the middle of the ceremony," Ray emphasized.

"What happened in the middle of the ceremony?" Linda asked.

"The preacher got to the part about anybody objecting to the marriage. All of a sudden three women jump up and accuse poor Penelope of being a witch. A group of men entered the church and grabbed Penelope right then and there and took her out into the woods. They all came back, but Penelope didn't. How weird is that?"

"Seriously? That's your idea of a story?" questioned Ken.

"I'm not finished, asshole. So anyway, she is said to haunt these woods seeking revenge."

"Holy crap, Ray. That story sucked. At least tell us what the men did to her."

"They killed her. Isn't that obvious?"

"But how?" Juanita asked.

"I don't know. The book didn't say. Who cares? She didn't come back and was never seen alive again. Use your freaking imaginations."

"Sucks dude. Just saying," Ken said.

They sat in silence for about three minutes, just watching the fire. Ken was about to begin a story he remembered from his childhood, but before he could make a sound, a shriek split the night air.

"What the hell was that? Sounded close." Ken said a little too loudly.

They were all unnerved by the sound. Biscuits began a low guttural growl.

Ray said, "It's probably a peacock."

Juanita looked at him in disgust. "A peacock? We just heard a scream, that made me pee my pants a second time by the way, and you think it was a peacock? Honey, sometimes you just amaze me. And not in a good way."

"No. Listen. Peacocks are said to make a loud noise that sounds like a woman screaming. I saw it on the National Geographic channel. All these peacocks were on some Greek island and screaming their little heads off. It's true," Ray insisted.

Just then the shriek sounded again, only closer. And it seemed angrier.

Biscuits was now barking and growling as if he were ready to defend his family. He was facing the woods directly behind the tents.

"Did you see that?" Linda asked.

"What? What did you see?" replied Ken.

"I saw something white move between the trees. Right there," Linda directed as she pointed at the same spot Biscuits was facing. "It was big. Like a person."

Ken grabbed a flashlight and walked towards the tree line. He was more than a bit afraid, but someone needed to take action. The sound had really unnerved him. It was very primal and almost human. He had a sinking feeling that this wasn't going to end well.

"Go with him Ray," Juanita insisted.

Ray, not wanting to be accused of being scared although he was, grabbed his own flashlight and scurried to catch up with Ken. He also had grabbed a short heavy branch from their woodpile. He didn't believe it would prove too effective, but believed it was better than being completely unarmed.

Ken's light was piercing and illuminated a fair amount of the treeline. He saw two or three pairs of eyes looking back at him at ground level. Obviously small animals not capable of the sound they had heard. Further into the woods he saw a flash of white between two trees. It confused him. It happened so fast. His first impression was that it was a woman in a white night gown.

Ray said, "I saw it too. It looked human. Right?"

"What would someone be doing out here running around in the woods? It's freaking dark as shit and there are wild animals and snakes to deal with. That would be insane," Ken declared.

"Well, we're out here. Is that insane?" Ray asked.

"I've got a 9mm Glock in my pocket. So no, it's not insane."

"A freaking Glock? Really?"

"Shhh. Be quiet. If Linda knew, she'd shoot me. And with my own gun," Ken whispered.

"I'm glad you're armed. All I got is this stupid stick. When I was a kid and I picked up a stick to play with, my mom would scream, 'drop it or you'll poke your eye out.' That woman scared the shit out of me most of the time."

Ken stopped and looked at Ray and laughed. Ray was the funniest guy he ever knew. He couldn't tell a good ghost story, but his tales about his childhood always made Ken laugh uproariously. "Let's go into the woods a bit. I'll pull my Glock to protect us and we'll get to the bottom of this."

Just as they began to enter the woods, both girls screamed for the guys to return to them. Biscuits had chosen the better part of valor and stayed with the women. He continued to growl as the men entered the woods. Even the dog knew that it wasn't a good idea.

Chapter Three

Rothrock

The next morning Cain sat alone in his office. Deke's photos of the deer were open on his computer desktop. He knew the wildlife in this area. Not one creature came to mind that could do what he was viewing on the screen. Definitely not without leaving bite marks or claw marks. Yet, here it was in high definition detail.

The phone rang. He picked it up slowly, as if in a fog. A man's voice that he recognized from the Centre County Sheriff's Office was telling him that a group of campers had been attacked in Rothrock State Park. He registered the words *fataltities, dog* and *survivor*. He then hung up the phone.

He called Mitch Salas, one of his subordinate wardens to meet him at the south entrance to Rothrock. He also told him to keep the media away if he could. He informed him that the Pennsylvania State Police were already heading to the park. His week just went from weird to worse.

As he hopped into his warden's SUV which was one of the best perks of his job, he had no idea that this call would relate to Deke's gruesome discovery. It did and he would find out soon enough.

Mitch Salas was as solid as they come. Smart, good looking, very professional. He had a wife and three little ones. He had been a warden for twelve years. It was his dream job.

He had seen death on the job on several occasions. One man was mauled to death by a bear, three others died of heart attacks during deer season, a hunter fell out of a deer stand and broke his neck and a child had been killed by a mountain lion several years back.

Upon arrival at the park entrance a state policeman stopped him. Mitch was in a marked warden SUV and the state cop wanted to warn him about the carnage.

"What the hell do you guys have out here in these woods? Something just turned three people and a dog into a pile of meat. I was first on the scene after a couple of hikers called it in. I couldn't even stay back there. What a mess," the trooper exclaimed.

"I'll go check it out. My boss is going to show up in a while. Could you tell him I went back? And where exactly is the incident located?" Mitch asked.

"About two hundred yards in on trailhead three. You'll see several state cars and an ambulance," the trooper stated.

"Oh, any survivors?" Mitch asked.

"One, but she was messed up mentally. When I got here she was just sitting on the ground rocking herself back and forth babbling something about somebody named Penelope and her monkey. Rocking and murmuring over and over. Penelope must be the name of the dead woman. Sad. Hope that poor girl recovers."

Mitch drove on to the spot. Rothrock was his main patrol area. If memory served him, there would be a clearing near where the trooper indicated the incident took place. Within eight minutes, he pulled up next to two state police vehicles.

He quickly located the ambulance and saw the EMTs working on a woman who appeared to be in her early thirties. She was bloodied, but seemed to be able to sit upright. She didn't wince at all the attention she was receiving. She didn't seem to be in pain. In fact, the look on her face would have to be described as vacant. Like she wasn't there.

A trooper saw Mitch and called him over.

"Are you taking lead on this?" asked the trooper.

"Either me or my boss. He'll be here in less than an hour. He was in his office at Canoe Creek when he got the call. So what's the story?"

The trooper began to walk him through it. They headed through the clearing that Mitch remembered and walked into the woods. Thirty yards in Mitch could see two troopers taking measurements and looking rather disgusted.

Mitch's guide showed him an arm, then a torso with no head, a leg, another torso. The tour continued in this fashion until Mitch said, "Okay, Trooper Wilkes, I get it. Pieces and parts everywhere. Any sense been made of it?"

"Holy shit, Warden…" The trooper looked at Mitch's name plate. "Warden Salas, that's your job, not ours. This isn't a homicide, it's an animal attack. Just look around."

Mitch did look around and was fighting his rising gorge. He saw a mass of flesh off to the side. It wasn't a limb or a head, so he asked, "what is that bit over there?"

"Oh yes. Let me show you," the trooper said as he stooped over a small mass of flesh lying on a downed tree trunk. He picked up a stick and used it to turn the object towards Mitch.

"Is that…a nipple?" Mitch asked, not really wanting the answer.

"Yep. And there is another one over there. The dead woman's breasts were, I dunno, pulled off her torso. Or chewed off or something. That's where you come in. Tell us what the hell happened."

Mitch looked at Wilkes. It was a pathetic look. The kind of look that screams *you must be freaking kidding me!* Bewilderment would have been too tame a word. Mitch hoped Cain had a better handle on this than he did.

Cain pulled up a few minutes later in his SUV. He got out and exchanged a few words with a trooper that was standing by the cars. Mitch watched, wishing he would hurry the hell up. He was eager for Cain to take over because he felt like he was completely out of his element.

"Hey Mitch," Cain said, "Fill me in."

Mitch bent over and threw up. He was embarrassed and humiliated by his reaction to this reality, but he had no control. He had been holding it down since Trooper Wilkes began his gory tour of the scene.

Wilkes saw what happened and rushed over.

"Hi. Name is Wilkes, and you are?"

"Chief Game Warden Cain."

"Your man is about the seventh person here to toss their cookies. I'm surprised he held out this long. Anyway, Chief Warden Cain, we have a bloody mess here and I am talking quite literally. I'll take you around while Warden Salas gets some fresh air."

Trooper Wilkes went through his guided tour once more. He pointed out the double mastectomy that was performed by God knows what. And also pointed out that they were missing a leg. Wilkes appeared almost more deeply saddened when he showed Cain the parts of the dead dog.

Cain thought the dog looked to be a fifty to sixty pound German Shepherd. At least that's what he imagined it would look like reassembled. It wasn't the people but the dog that made him lock in on the connection to Deke's deer.

He immediately began to think that the humans would yield better clues than the canine. After all, the dog was covered in fur and made things difficult, but humans bruise and show damage much more clearly. That's where he would focus.

Mitch caught up with him. "What are you looking at, Warden Cain?"

"Look, Mitch. There's bruising around the wrist of this arm. Like something was holding it. Obviously not rope or restraints, but something had a grip here. See?"

"Yessir," the subordinate replied.

They investigated the site for three more hours. Cain's conclusion was simple. There were no bites, claw marks or deep scratches. No knife or blade marks, neither plain or serrated had been employed to take apart the victims.

What was apparent were several areas of bruising around wrists, ankles, elbows and necks. Something strong but soft had laid ahold of these people and their dog. Something strong enough to crush bone and pull bones and sinew apart.

The only animal evidence were some hairs found on the victims and caught in the trees and vegetation surrounding the kill zone. They could be from anything. The area also seemed to be trampled and flattened pretty thoroughly, but nothing stood out such as paw prints or boots for that matter.

"You know the strangest thing I see here, Mitch?" Cain asked.

"No sir. The whole damn thing seems strange from start to finish."

"But think about this. These people have been dead for hours. Fresh meat for all the little forest animals. Yet there is no sign of even a nibble on these corpses. Just a missing leg."

"Maybe the survivor scared all the other animals away?" Salas offered.

At that moment one of the medical examiner's crew passed by and said, "look, I got me a fresh bag of titties," as he held up an evidence bag which obviously held the poor deceased woman's breasts.

Cain and Salas just shook their heads that someone could be so callous after witnessing this carnage.

Chapter 4

More Questions Than Answers

Cain had his hands full. Two days after the scene was cleared and all evidence collected, he called a meeting of all his officers at the headquarters in Canoe Creek. It also served as the park's welcome center. It was an 18th century cabin. Rather large for the time period. There were four distinct rooms. A small kitchen occupied one, a small room that had been a bedroom, the bathroom and the huge main office. The original cooking area and large stone fireplace were now located in the main office. He would be cramming forty-one people in the main office for their meeting. Five wardens would be absent due to court appearances.

Forty-one men and five women covered the entire western half of Pennsylvania from Potter, Clinton, Centre, Huntingdon and Fulton Counties to the Ohio border, and from the New York border south to Maryland and West Virginia. Thirty-one counties in all.

During certain seasons such as deer season, the budget allowed for additional part-time help. Forty-six full-timers and Cain were simply not enough manpower to patrol those forests. Everyone knew it, even the bad guys who took advantage of the manpower shortage, but unbelievably they still made several hundred arrests and ticketed thousands of folks per annum.

Cain knew he had a great group of wardens. Today he needed to bring them up to speed on the Rothrock situation. He wanted to see if anything about this case was familiar to anyone. He hoped that maybe his people had encountered similar attacks that could help shed some light on what they were dealing with.

He began with Deke's story and the trail cam photos. Then he followed with the dismembered deer from the photos. And finally he showed his people the gruesome attack scene photos and told them what he knew.

He couldn't call it a crime scene because he and the state police had agreed that it had to be an animal attack. The most bizarre one he had ever encountered, but an animal attack was the only thing that made sense.

During his presentation, the attack scene photos segment specifically, several of his wardens stepped out. The photos were upsetting. Once all had returned he told them, "those were just photos, folks. The real thing was ten times worse. So my question for you today is, do you know what did this? Any ideas at all would be helpful."

A few said it had to be a bear. That was quickly explained away by the lack of claw and teeth marks, tracks and scat. No indicators whatsoever except a few hairs.

Some guessed mountain lion and that was dismissed for all the same reasons. Coyotes, feral dogs and humans were eliminated as well.

One warden raised his hand and Cain called on him. He stood and introduced himself, although everyone knew him. He was Donald Denali. Everyone he knew called him *Moose Tracks*, after the Hershey ice cream flavor. He was one of the older wardens. Cain thought he was in his late forties or early fifties.

"Sir, I seem to recall an incident during the nineties where a couple of backpackers were found torn apart over in Gallitzin. I don't think it was ever resolved."

Cain turned to Warden Michael Kelso who patrolled the Gallitzin forests. "Mike, sound familiar?"

"Before my time sir, but I can look it up," he replied.

"Sir," continued Denali. "There was also a similar incident in the early eighties in Moshannon. A fisherman was found dismembered and disemboweled. If I remember correctly, it was attributed to a bear attack. The problem with that was the wardens in charge of that investigation were stumped as to why a black bear would have acted so viciously and how there could be no evidence of the bear's presence other than the dead fisherman."

"What do you mean *acted so viciously*?" someone in the group called out.

Denali responded, "Black bears are lazy buggers. They don't expend any more energy than necessary to complete a task. The fisherman would have died, or been incapacitated quickly. So why did the bear continue to, quite literally, tear him limb from limb? It doesn't make sense."

Warden Jane Doreemer was heard by all saying, "this is freaking me out."

The room broke into laughter. It was what was needed to lighten the mood for at least a few moments. The psychological impact of the photos was palpable. Cain could see signs of strain, fear and revulsion as he looked around the room, yet these good people weren't on the scene. Being there was so much worse.

A warden stood up. He was relatively new to the group. His name was Tony Landolfi.

"I have a question, sir," Tony said. "Where does the screaming woman in the photo figure into all this? We've talked about the damage to the deer and the people and their dog, but we've skipped over the significance of her appearance."

"You're right, Tony. She's our mystery guest. And the other creepy factoid is the survivor's words when we got on scene. What we got out of her was *Penelope and her monkey*. And since the dead woman was named Juanita, we are at a loss as to who Penelope is. It could be another victim for all we know," Cain answered.

"One more thing," Landolfi went on. "You said a few hairs were found. What kind?"

"I talked to the wildlife zoologist/biologist at Penn State who does this sort of work for us and he's stumped. He believes the hairs are primate, but not like any he's seen before. He's still doing tests. That could be Penelope's monkey's hair. Which would lead us to, once again, entertain that we have a missing victim and her pet."

Landolfi pressed on, "Warden Cain, you still haven't really explained the creepy looking woman in the trail pictures."

"That's because I can't Tony. I do not have a single clue where she fits in. Any ideas?"

The room was silent as Landolfi sat down.

"Dammit, Cain. Have you forgotten what I told you the other day?"

Every head whipped around as well as Cain's.

The group found themselves staring at Deke Humboldt. He had snuck in the side door of the room when the questions were being asked.

"Meet Deke Humboldt, our answer to Daniel Boone in these parts," Cain explained.

"Aww, hell no! Daniel Boone's a faggot. I'm more like Davy Crockett. Now there's a frontiersman. Glad to make your acquaintance," Deke said to the group.

A few wardens laughed or smiled knowingly. It seems every area has a Deke.

Cain explained, "Deke has a theory, which makes sense to him and, coincidentally, ties into our survivor's comments. Go ahead, Deke."

Deke weaved his ghostly tale for the group to enjoy and identified himself as the source of the trail cam photos and the chronicler of the dismembered eight point buck. When he was done, you could have heard a pin drop. Deke had the ability to enthrall an audience.

"So you see, the survivor is telling us who to look for. Good ol' Penelope is up to no good," Deke concluded.

Cain reclaimed control of the meeting. "Any questions?"

"Not a question sir, but a point of information," Warden Salas spoke up. "Once word of this incident got out over in Centre County, several people called me to tell me of incidents from years back with similar circumstances. They have always been called bear attacks, but anyone with the truthful accounts of what occurred have always been doubtful. I think we should revisit all the bear attacks, say for the last one hundred years and see if we have a pattern."

A murmur coursed through the crowd.

Warden Miller stood up. "Excuse me, but certainly the creature isn't one hundred years old. Why go back that far?"

Salas defended his point. "Maybe not a single individual, but a thriving population may have existed for years. We are encroaching on different species' habitats with alarming frequency. Maybe we did with these creatures. Whatever they are."

Warden Harold Muncy stood. "Come on folks. We keep saying creature like this is some damn sci-fi movie. It has to be a familiar animal were dealing with. And most certainly a bear. Why are we making this out to be a mystery? It's the only logical answer. And sorry old timer," he said looking at Deke, "it sure as hell ain't a ghost." Then he sat down feeling content that he had had his say.

Deke mumbled, "little chicken shit bastard." Several of the nearby wardens snorted and laughed. Muncy wasn't overly popular with the group.

Cain said, "Okay, Salas has a good idea. We each are too busy for such a project, but I have a college intern starting next week. That will be one of her priorities.

The meeting continued and focused on new rules concerning hunting and fishing quotas, newly designated protected species and the new fining system for citations.

Two hours later the meeting broke up and the wardens could head home to their own districts or stick around for coffee and donuts, which Cain paid for out of his own pocket. He didn't mind. He appreciated each one of these men and women.

The state was very stingy in outfitting the department. Pennsylvania supplied uniforms and a badge. That was it. Each officer had to supply their own gun, cuffs, holster, bullets and vehicle.

They could buy a warden's hat if they chose to. Most did. The Smokey Bear hat was a cherished sign and tradition of the service. Some preferred baseball caps with the department patch on it, especially if working on the water. Either one was paid for by the officer.

The thirty-one counties in the Western Pennsylvania District had twelve vehicles. Three were permanently sidelined for repairs until budget items could be allocated. Cain was ROC so he had the newest SUV in the fleet. Salas had one also. The other seven were spread out. Cain wasn't even sure which officers had them. Everyone else used their own trucks or four-wheel drive vehicles.

Pennsylvania wouldn't provide any more vehicles, but stipulated all vehicles used by officers had to be four-wheel drive. The state was very free with other people's money. There was a gas allowance that was adequate as long as gas didn't go over three dollars a gallon again. No one was in this for the money and perks.

It was one of the reasons Cain felt very protective of his officers. They were dedicated to the mission. They were loyal to an ideal. They were a dying breed.

He didn't know how true that last statement would become.

Chapter 5

Some Things Satisfy And Some Don't

Two weeks passed by and many things transpired. The first of which seems minor on the surface. Two dogs were reported missing. Two separate incidents involving campers at Rothrock. It happens several times a year. Campers are told not to let Rover off his leash, but they don't listen.

The usual explanation is mountain lions, bears, raccoons or snakes. Also dogs, believe it or not, can become disoriented in amongst so many smells and sounds which they are unaccustomed. Sometimes Rover shows up days or weeks later and sometimes not.

The wildlife zoologist/biologist Doctor Harold Slocum from Penn State main campus who was examining the hairs from the scene of the attack, broke his identification down like this:

Kingdom: Animalia
Phylum: Chordata
Class: Mammalia
Order: Primates
Suborder: Haplorhini
Parvorder: Catarrhini
Superfamily: Hominidae
Genus: Indeterminate

When Cain received the report in the mail, he was dumbfounded. This wasn't at all satisfactory. For one, he would have appreciated an email with an attachment, since the nature of this case was rather urgent.

And two, this left the door wide open for people to take the survivor's comments very seriously. Cain wasn't ready to investigate the *Penelope and her monkey* reference.

For the uninitiated, Doctor Slocum's report was saying the hairs belonged to the Hominid family which was made up of humans, gorillas, orangutans and chimpanzees. But being specific wasn't possible.

Cain felt a call was in order, so he made it.

The conversation didn't go as he had hoped.

"Dr. Slocum, thank you for your expert opinion regarding our hair samples. We always appreciate your help."

Before Cain could draw his next breath, Slocum cut in. "It doesn't satisfy, does it, Warden? I've left you with a big old mess, haven't I?" He continued. "Let's cut to the chase. It resembles gorilla hair, but it's not. It has a slightly orange pigmentation like orangutan hair, but it's not. It even shares some of the same protein structure of chimpanzee hair, but it's not. The only definitive statement that I feel I can make, and this is more opinion than fact, is that it is not human."

"So it is a great ape of some sort. That certainly doesn't satisfy."

"Actually, I didn't really say that either," the doctor protested.

"Doctor Slocum, when you placed it in the Hominidae classification, that is exactly what you were saying. Great ape," Cain declared rather testily.

"I don't want my name associated with any of this, Warden Cain. I will deny everything," the doctor declared.

"What is your problem, Slocum? You're acting irrational."

"Warden Cain, my first position on a college staff was at the University of Oregon in Eugene, Oregon. The campus is only fifty to eighty miles away from several major forested areas: Mt. Hood National Forest, Umpqua National Forest, Williamette National Forest, Siuslaw National Forest. Are you getting my drift?

"I was young and naïve and people sought me out for my expert opinion. It went to my head and I got sucked into the culture of Bigfoot that exists out there. It almost ruined me. I went underground for a few years and then was fortunate enough to be hired at Penn State.

"I won't falsify research, or misidentify anything that comes across my desk because it is ultimately the most beautiful truth there is. It is science in all its glory to be able to so completely know God's creation. But I won't get drawn into this nightmare again."

Whoa, thought Cain, a *scientist that believes in God.*

He then spoke aloud. "Doctor, I understand and will protect your reputation, but I need an answer. Just between you and me, do these hair samples closely relate to the Bigfoot studies being done in the Northwest?"

"Yes, they are the same creature," he admitted.

"Doctor, to help my men stay safe and keep the public safe, what can you tell me about these things?"

"They don't exist." Then the doctor hung up.

A good thing that happened during the previous two weeks was the internship. Ellen Obermiller was the intern's name. She was a surprise to Cain in that he expected a twenty year old know nothing college kid. What he ended up with was a thirty-three year old, fairly attractive grad student.

She had noted on her application for the internship that she was one-sixteenth Native American. Specifically, she belonged to the Delaware tribe through her great-grandmother. She had beautiful dark hair with a slightly reddish sheen which she wore straight down to the middle of her back. Cain found her figure quite comely. Her smile was her best feature though. It lit up her face and whatever room she occupied at the time.

Cain was forty and had never been married. Several women tried mightily to change that, but none were up to the challenge. Cain was married to his job and in six years would be eligible for full retirement. That was his goal and yet the thought of retirement scared him. He loved what he was doing.

The first task she was given was to bring the office filing system up to date. She jumped right in and had things pretty well caught up in about a week and a half. She worked overtime on the project.

Cain told her there was nothing beyond the small stipend that she was receiving, but she didn't care. She loved a challenge and told him she had nothing better to do with her time.

Cain noted that. Maybe when her internship was completed he would entertain asking her out. Currently, however, that would be an ethics violation. And Cain had deep pockets when it came to ethics. He was a very moral man and was greatly respected in every circle he moved in.

The next assignment he gave Ellen was compiling the reports on the bear attacks. He brought her up to speed on the attacks, but spared her the photographs. He gave her tips on what to look for and told her to report her findings only to him. The department couldn't afford any leaks to the media.

After four days, she came to Cain with what she had found. She was nothing if not efficient. Although the case was considered to be urgent, he never expected such quick results.

"Agent Cain, I've found eleven suspicious cases in one hundred years."

"It's Warden Cain, not agent. Please let me see what you have found."

She handed over her notes and case files.

He knew that bear attacks were actually a rare occurrence. And overwhelmingly bear attacks were not fatal. What made the eleven cases that Ellen found so remarkable was that they were all fatalities and several involved multiple deaths caused by dismemberment. This was not typical bear behavior.

"Thank you, Ellen. Now I have a rather difficult request. I need you to dig for any supporting files that might have photos, medical examiner reports, eyewitness accounts, survivors of any kind. Do you follow?"

"Yes, Agent...I mean Warden Cain. Now that we have a pool of suspicious attacks, you want me to dig deeper. Anything else?"

"Have you eaten lunch?" he asked.

"No. Not yet."

"Do you want to split a pizza?" he boldly put forth.

"Will this be a lunch date?" she inquired with the hint of a smile.

He wanted to be cool without saying no. "I don't care what you want to call it. I'm hungry."

"I'll get right on it." She partially turned and said, "oh, pepperoni acceptable?"

"Who do you know who doesn't like pepperoni?" he joked.

"My ex-husband."

"And that, I presume, is why he is your ex," he continued trying to be humorously cute.

"That and the regular beatings he gave me," she laughed and finished her turn and walked over to the phone book on her desk.

He had no idea if she was serious or not. What kind of dirtbag beats his wife? He knew the answer of course. He had arrested several wife beaters in the camping areas over the years.

He recalled a man who fractured his wife's skull with a skillet, right in front of their two kids. When he arrived, three other campers were sitting on top of him and an EMT unit was already on site treating her.

Cain's blood boiled that day. If he could have gotten away with it, he would have buried the guy up to his neck and let the forest creatures have at him. This was a particularly dark thought for Cain. He was a devout Christian and it shamed him to feel this way, but men who hurt women or children drew him to a dark place.

The woman survived and reconciled with her husband. In less than a year she was dead. It still saddened him to think of those kids growing up without a mommy and their dad in prison for murder. He prayed for them for years.

If she was joking, then he needed to tell her not to. It was no laughing matter to him or anyone else associated with that reality. He just had to make sure he didn't come on too strong.

Thirty minutes later, they were eating pizza at his desk and enjoying pleasant conversation.

She changed the subject like this. "Your friend, Deke, stopped by the other day while you were out. He told me it wasn't necessary to tell you or I would have. He's quite a character, isn't he?"

"He's the definition of character. He has more personality than Robin Williams had and that's saying a whole lot. He really is the funniest man I know."

"How long have you known him?"

"About nineteen years. I met him the first or second year that I was a warden. His knowledge of the forest is second to none," he informed her.

"How is he as far as his knowledge on ghosts that roam the forest?" She had a cute little smirk on her face.

"Well, that would be Deke to a T. He has valuable knowledge, but you kind of have to peel away the…uh."

"Bullshit?" she finished as a question.

"Yep. You hit that nail right on the head. He likes drama and tall tales. He loves a mystery and what we currently have going on here fits that description. He is in his element and the old ghost tale and his trail cam photo has him all excited."

"What do you think? Off the record, of course."

"I think a closer look needs to be taken at the evidence. If this isn't a bear attack, then we need to identify what it truly is before someone else gets hurt. So how's your pizza?"

Ellen picked up on the conversation ending segue. She didn't push it any farther.

At quitting time, which was five o'clock, Cain asked Ellen, "Did Warden Muncy call in this afternoon when I stepped out?"

"No, sir. I would have told you. There are no messages on the machine either. Were you expecting his call?"

"Yes. He's one of my floaters. I use him wherever I need him depending on workload, circumstances, vacation and things like that. He was going to have another look at Rothrock for me. Maybe we'll come in tomorrow and have a message from him. Goodnight, Ellen."

She smiled. "Goodnight, Warden Cain.

They both drove away thinking how easily they got along. It was obviously good for both of them. Ellen liked him and she had an inkling that he reciprocated. She knew the perils of an office romance and would be extremely cautious.

Chapter 6

A Dying Breed

When Cain showed up at work the next day, Ellen was already there digging deeper into the supposed bear attacks. As he entered the office Ellen bounced up from her old gray metal desk with a stack of messages.

"Your dentist called to confirm your appointment next Monday. Just curious why you gave them your work number?"

"I'm always working."

"Okay. Warden Sankowski called and needs permission to rent watercraft to pull up illegal fishing traps. Warden Salas needs to get his SUV serviced and wants to know where you want him to take it since your run-in with the guy at the State Police motor pool. And Warden Muncy has not made contact with us."

"Us?"

"Well, I work for you now. So you and I are a *we* or an *us*, depending on the proper grammatical usage," she beamed with confidence that she had made her case.

"Okay. Why don't *us*, meaning *you*, call Sankowski and tell him to go ahead, but keep it under three hundred dollars. Call Salas and tell him to get his vehicle service done at Walmart. And I, meaning *me*, will go and confirm with my dentist. Do *we* understand?"

"Wow. You seemed like such a nice man up to now. I guess I, meaning *me*, will have to adjust," she said, pretending to be offended.

Cain couldn't help but to walk away with a smile. All the other women he had dated for years had little or no sense of humor. Ellen, however, was almost perfect. It was early, but he really couldn't let her get away.

He wasn't off the phone with his dentist's office more than five minutes when Ellen informed him that Warden Muncy's wife was on line three. He knew this couldn't be good.

"Good morning, Vera. How may I help you?"

"Harold didn't come home last night. He doesn't answer his cell either. I'm worried," she told him.

"Okay, Vera. I'll run over to Rothrock and check on him. He is probably in an area with no cell reception and sleeping in his car."

"He always comes home, Warden Cain. Always," she insisted.

"I'll check it out right now. It'll be a while before I get back to you. His last known location was forty-five minutes away," he told her so she wouldn't worry. Of course, by the sound of her voice she was concerned, but not worried the way other wives sounded under similar circumstances.

"I'm sorry to be such a bother."

"Vera, my plans were to go up there anyway. No problem. I'll call you later. Or he will." With that he said goodbye and hung up.

Cain was now more concerned than Muncy's wife. He did not like the feel of this at all.

"Ellen, I'm headed to Rothrock. Have Warden Salas meet me there as soon as possible," he ordered. He liked having someone with whom to delegate his communication chores. Normally he would be on the phone talking, text messaging, emailing or on the radio communicating and coordinating. He needed to be on the road, not wasting his time playing secretary. The budget crisis had to end soon. He needed clerical support, even if only part-time.

Salas was waiting for him at the western entrance to the forest. He was right under the big beautiful carved sign on which the state didn't mind spending money. They spent over a thousand, maybe more, for each sign that stood next to the twenty or so authorized entrances to this forest, but he couldn't get the equipment or manpower that he needed.

"How did you get here so fast? I thought you were getting your car serviced," Cain said.

"Already done. Walmart was a great idea. They were quick and cheap. Better than those ten minute lube places that are all over creation," Salas responded.

"Yeah. What a joke. Do any of those places ever take less than forty minutes," Cain added, "Here's the scoop, Muncy is missing. I had him come over here two days ago. He didn't make it home last night and his wife Vera says he always comes home. She's concerned and so am I. So consider this a search and rescue on the down low. I don't want to push the panic button yet."

Salas left his car at the entrance and hopped in with Cain. They would start with trailhead three and work the areas in order after that. They needed to be methodical and thorough.

Rothrock is densely populated by deciduous and coniferous trees. Deciduous, or broad leafed trees, are clearly in the majority. It is home to almost every species of wildlife that one can think of within the borders of the state of Pennsylvania.

Mountain lions, black bears, rattlesnakes and copperheads are the species that man needs to steer clear of within the forest. An occasional wild boar may be encountered as well. The only other concern would be rabid creatures, chief among them being the raccoon.

Cain had a sinking feeling something else was in the forest as well. Doctor Slocum had him officially on edge and open to new possibilities. He hadn't yet shared that conversation with anyone. He was hoping he wouldn't have to.

Aside from the seriousness of their task, Cain was reveling in the changing leaves. The reds were stunning, the oranges almost neon where the sun broke through. The golds provided a regal ambience to the once green forest. This was autumn the way countless poets and writers of prose have described it for hundreds of years.

He wondered if autumn was this spectacular in other countries around the world. This season was the season to treasure. The last gasps of life played out in beautiful colors. The stark dead contrast of winter ahead.

"Cain, look!" Salas yelled.

Cain stopped his SUV and blinked at what Salas had noticed. Muncy, as his floating warden, had one of the other marked SUVs provided by the state. What they were staring at was the door of that SUV lying along the side of the road, partially propped up by a large rock.

They got out of their vehicle and stood staring at the door in complete bewilderment. The glass was broken out of the door window and the hinges, for lack of a better word, were mangled. The side of the door was stoved in at several spots. Long gouges in the paint suggested it had been dragged along the ground. The rest of the vehicle was nowhere in sight.

Salas spoke up. "Sir, is that blood on the window frame?"

Cain stepped forward and got down on his haunches. He could see it was dried, but blood would be his first guess. He said over his shoulder, "radio the State Police and a rescue unit. I think we have a situation on our hands."

Salas returned to the vehicle and did as he was told. Cain pulled his cellphone from his pocket. Thank goodness he had one bar of cell reception. He called Ellen and told her to contact Wardens Smith and Sorenson. Both were in adjacent counties. He wanted them here as soon as possible.

She asked if he was okay. He told her he was and that if Vera Muncy called, tell her they were still searching and nothing else.

"Is Warden Muncy alright?" she asked.

"I don't know, Ellen. There could be a problem. You must be tight lipped about this. Especially with Vera."

"I understand perfectly, Warden Cain. You can count on me."

"Call me Jeremy."

"Call me Ellie."

They hung up having made a minor concession to familiarity. In the long run it could be huge, he hoped. Now back to a sober reality.

They picked up tire tracks going deeper into the woods past trailhead three. Cain and Salas weren't waiting for their back up. The urgency to find Muncy was insatiable. Inactivity wasn't an option.

They drove slowly and saw gouged and peeled bark evidenced by trees closest to the trail, as if a vehicle had careened off of them. Tracks were plentiful off to the sides of the trail on both sides.

Salas observed, "he was having a hard time maintaining control, by the looks of it. Why wouldn't he just stop?"

"Maybe something was chasing him," Cain said pensively.

"Seriously, Sir?"

"Well, what's your explanation…oh shit. Look."

Cain stopped talking and stared straight ahead.

Salas did likewise.

Muncy's SUV was on its side facing away from them.

Both hopped out and approached the car cautiously. Working their way around to the front, they saw that the front windshield was missing. There was no sign of Muncy. Yet.

Cain radioed in their location.

Salas yelled, "Muncy!"

Cain joined, "Harold, where are you?"

An hour later they were hoarse from yelling. The first of their reinforcements had arrived in fifteen minutes. Two state troopers and an ambulance crew were on scene. Cain explained what they had already found. All said they took notice of the door lying out near the trailhead.

Smith and Sorenson were coming from different directions, but both said they would be there in fifteen minutes. They would then have enough help to start to scour the woods.

An EMT walked over to Cain, "Warden, there is a considerable amount of blood in the front of that vehicle.

We need to find this guy, fast." Cain knew that he was right, but deep down he thought it was too late.

A blood trail didn't start directly next to the car. Twenty feet away a trooper found a smashed down area of vegetation and a lot of blood. The trail began.

"Why wasn't there a blood trail from the car to here?" Salas asked.

Cain replied, "He was thrown."

"But sir, the vehicle is facing in the opposite direction," Salas pointed out.

"I didn't say that it was the vehicle that threw him. Did I?"

Salas was taken aback by Cain's response. But he was starting to wonder about what could be happening here. None of it made sense.

The blood trail was followed by the group. The first body part was Muncy's head. Even in the autumn chill, the flies couldn't resist showing up for their gory feast.

From this location the group spread out to find the rest of their fallen comrade. Warden Smith, newly arrived on the scene, found the torso, sans legs and arms.

Within ten minutes two arms and a leg were found. Another hour of searching did not yield the missing limb.

Trooper Alvarez asked Cain, "what in the hell do you guys have out here? First the hikers and now one of your own?"

"Cain ignored the question from the trooper. "Salas, get the camera out of the glove compartment. We need to document this before it gets dark."

Alvarez approached Cain, "do you need our crime lab team?"

"No," Cain responded, "this is still in the animal attack category as far as I can tell. But thanks. We could use you guys to stick around though. It might be dark soon and having a few more armed companions would be reassuring."

"Sure thing," Alvarez responded. "I'll get it cleared."

The ambulance crew gave Cain and Salas their condolences for having lost a comrade. They then packed up and pulled out. They would soon be replaced by a team from the coroner's office to transfer the found pieces of Harold Muncy to the morgue.

"Warden Salas, can you finish up here? I have a long drive ahead of me. I need to go tell Vera Muncy that she is a widow. The state cops will remain with you, Smith and Sorenson until the scene is cleared."

"Yes sir. Good luck."

Chapter 7

The Widow

The drive to see Muncy's widow was the highlight of his day. The reason was that he had called Ellen to tell her what he was doing and to lock up the office when she left for the day.

She insisted on going with him.

"Jeremy, you need a woman with you. I can be a better shoulder to cry on in circumstances like these. A woman wants to share her pain with another woman. No offense."

"None taken. I can't pay you any more than what you're already receiving and this would be way beyond the call of duty," he insisted.

"And I told you before, I have nothing better to do. Really, you can buy me dinner though, since I'll be hungry at some point soon," she suggested. "That way you need not feel so bad."

"Okay, but on my salary it's going to have to be fast food. And Ellie, I really appreciate this. I'll be by to pick you up in about fifty minutes. And then we'll continue on. The Muncy's live about forty-five minutes beyond the office."

"I'll be ready," she assured him.

He picked her up and as they drove they talked like they had known each other for years. Had anyone been with them, they never would have guessed the sad mission they were on.

The end of their pleasant drive was upon them and Cain pulled into the Muncy's driveway which led up to a small split level. The house was white with black shutters, a sprawling front yard and a basketball hoop along the side of the driveway. It was a snapshot of middle America.

They knocked. As soon as Vera opened the door she knew.

"He's dead, isn't he, Warden Cain?" Vera blurted out.

"Yes, Vera. I'm so sorry," he responded.

"Well, I guess I should invite you in," she said in an emotionless fashion.

Was it shock? Cain wondered. Or did she somehow already know? A psychic bond of some sort. This was not the reaction they were expecting.

"Who's this?" Vera asked.

"I'm Ellie, the intern."

"Hello Ellie, the intern. I'm Vera, the widow."

Vera's demeanor was throwing both Cain and Ellie off script.

"Sorry, Warden Cain, if you're expecting a flood of tears or some such nonsense, you will be disappointed. Harold and I had an understanding after all these years. We were roommates. Even friends, by some definitions, but love ran its course years ago.

"He was a difficult man. Mentally abusive at times. I mean I stilled worried about him when he was late, or in this case, missing. But mostly because we had fallen into a comfortable rhythm or pattern for our kids and grand kids.

"We often joked that the first to die is the winner. Thinking about it now, that was wrong. I believe maybe I'm going to be the winner. How did he die anyway?"

Cain looked at Ellen and she at him. "Sit down, Vera. Even if you didn't love the man, this is going to be difficult to hear."

He went on to describe the series of events that led up to the discovery of his body. And then he described the condition of the body as gently as he could. As soon as he talked about dismemberment, Vera's hand flew up to cover her mouth.

Cain could see tears forming in her eyes. He believed she cared for her husband more than she had realized. There was a certain indignity to Harold's death. Or maybe she was more worried about her children and grandchildren. It was hard to tell.

Jeremy Cain had never wanted to leave a home more than he did this one. Vera had set everything on its ear. Grief stricken wives are difficult enough to handle, but you knew in what direction to move the conversation and you knew that compassion and comfort were needed. With Vera, he wasn't sure how to act.

Ellie was no better off. She came prepared to be a strong shoulder to cry on. Or even cry with the widow. She wasn't expecting this cold strangeness. Vera seemed so detached emotionally that Ellie was surprised that she had been worried about her husband's absence at all.

"Vera, we'll leave you to the sad task of notifying your children, unless you need our help with that," he offered, hoping that she wouldn't accept.

"Warden Cain, you and your girlfriend here were kind to come, thank you," Vera said.

Ellie immediately spoke up, "No, Mrs. Muncy, we're not a couple."

Vera replied, "Well, dear, you should be. Now thank you for coming and drive safely." She stood and walked to the front door and opened it.

That was their cue to leave and it couldn't have come sooner. Cain was ready to bolt. Ellie hesitated. Cain thought to himself, *come on woman, let's get the hell out of here.*

"What did you mean by *we should be?*" asked Ellie.

"The way you interact and look at each other is the textbook definition of attraction. It's obvious. Harold and I had that once, years ago of course, but we had it. Enjoy it dear. It doesn't last."

Cain wasn't listening to any more of her musings. He went out the door. Ellie followed.

They drove back to the office to pick up Ellie's car. On the way Cain pulled into a McDonald's and bought Ellie dinner. She ordered a Quarter Pounder and a small Diet Coke. He had nothing.

The drive seemed unbelievably long for both of them. The comfort they shared earlier was replaced by awkwardness. She ate her meal in silence and he had nothing to say.

Once at the office, she opened her door and then turned to him, "are you mad because of what she said about us?"

"No. Not mad. Embarrassed."

"Don't be. She was right. We would make a nice couple. Goodnight." She jumped out of the car and shut the door before Cain could respond. She then got into her own car and drove away.

Warden Jeremy Cain sat in his SUV and didn't know whether to shit or go blind. That's the way his dad always put it when you found yourself at a loss for words or action. But Cain did do one thing. He smiled from ear to ear.

Salas, Smith and Sorenson and the two troopers were ready to wrap things up. It was too dark to get anything more done. As they walked back to their cars they heard a shriek. It was piercing and sounded like a woman, but they all agreed it had to have been an animal. Sound carries and is sometimes distorted in the forest.

The wardens had taken a ration of crap from the state troopers all afternoon and early evening. One of them asked if it was a requirement that all wardens had to have a last name that started with the letter S. The second stater got a little more caustic when he asked how it felt to *almost* be a cop. The other trooper shut him down and said that it wasn't cool, but it was already out there and couldn't be taken back. Salas wondered if this was how all the troopers felt.

Salas saw something white flitting between the trees. He kept his mouth shut. Every nerve in his body tingled and fear overcame him. He didn't even know why. He just knew he wanted to leave that scene behind. And there was one other thing he wished for: daylight.

It sat on a log by itself in a clearing two miles away from where Warden Salas and his group had been. Until the shrieking woman had found it, it lived a life of solitude. Except when the urge to mate overcame it. Then it sought others of its kind, which were few and far between.

Normally solitary and peaceful, the creature would fly into an uncontrollable rage at the presence of the shrieking woman. Its primitive mind knew that the unbridled anger was not its own. It knew that it was her anger that was channeled through its mind and body. It had no choice when it happened, which added a little fury of its own.

It also sensed her anger was focused, usually on one victim, but there was always collateral damage if the target was accompanied by others. It didn't understand what collateral damage was, but was able to realize the other surrounding creatures were in as much danger as her target. She usually had sufficient rage for all.

It remembered that the group with the growling creature did have one member that was not destroyed like the others. It did not sense mercy, as far as it understood such things, was at play. It just seemed that after four creatures were torn asunder, her anger ebbed and she lost interest.

It disliked losing control. Each rage episode left it famished and weakened. Hunger was the only thing on its mind at the moment. It raised its latest prize and gently removed some cloth that still stuck to it. Then, with a longing groan, it took a huge bite out of a leg that had once belonged to Warden Muncy.

Chapter 8

A Puzzling Discovery

Ellie was in the office before Jeremy. She wanted to be a valuable asset and figured that if she became the best Girl Friday she could possibly be, then Warden Cain would have to be impressed. She reasoned that he normally was the only occupant of this office and two had to be better than one, so her efforts couldn't go unnoticed.

She began by brewing coffee. She then attacked the chore of cleaning the office starting with the bathroom. She was a human dynamo with boundless reserves of energy. She was also fueled by the desire to make Cain happy. She was beginning to fall for him.

She knew her comments as she was leaving Jeremy's car were rather bold. Ellie hoped that didn't turn him off in any way. When she saw him this morning she would act as if she had never said a thing. The ball was completely in his court.

An hour later she heard his car engine as he pulled into his space. Or so she thought. She anticipated him walking through the front door, but instead Deke walked in.

"Well hey, little lady. You don't have to look so disappointed. You're going to give a man a complex. Who were you expecting? Brad Pitt?"

"Sorry, Deke. I'm just busy cleaning," she covered.

"No. Wait a minute. You weren't expecting Brad, even though he no longer answers to Angelina. You were expecting one Jeremy Cain. You've been smitten, haven't you?"

She turned twelve shades of red and couldn't come up with a response. Deke gave a hearty laugh. "Don't worry, Ellie. I won't tell. To be honest, I figure you're exactly what that boy needs."

"I guess I'm guilty as charged. I figured, since I'm not a good cook I would win him over with becoming an invaluable asset around here," she truthfully revealed.

"Sweetie, girls as pretty as you don't need to know how to cook. So when is that lucky boy going to show up?"

She shrugged her shoulders. She had no clue what his schedule was.

Deke continued, "I heard Muncy was killed. That was a shame. His family was one of the oldest in these parts. Same way with that hiker, Ken McKenna. His family was original to the early settlement here too. We're gonna run out of founding families if this keeps up."

Ellie really wanted to get back to her cleaning so she prodded. "So what brings you in today? Anything I can help you with?"

"Sure, Cain called me last night to see if I'd poke around the two attack scenes this morning to see if I would pick up on anything that could have been missed. And I did. Here."

"What's this?" she asked as she took a gallon Ziploc bag from his hand.

"That, Miss Ellie, is a 9mm Glock pistol. It was near the scene where the hikers had been killed. It has recently been fired, but I don't know how many times. The clip is empty, though. So somebody was shooting at something."

"Wasn't that spot, from what I read, thoroughly combed by the state police and the wardens? How did they miss it?" she asked.

"In all fairness, it was under some scrub and thirty feet or so from the main attack site. And I used something to which they didn't have access. I used a metal detector," Deke said proudly.

"Wait a minute," Ellie interjected. "My brother owns a Glock. Isn't it made of plastic or something? How did your metal detector pick up on it?"

"Not plastic, little lady. Polymer. And it still has enough metal parts to be detected. Betsy is very sensitive."

"Who is Betsy?" she inquired with some confusion.

"She's my metal detector. I name all my favorite tools."

"You need a woman."

"Had one. Too much trouble. No offense."

"None taken. I'll give the gun to Jeremy when he gets here."

"Okay, Miss Ellie. I gotta go. Tell your boyfriend to call me." And he abruptly turned around and exited before she could react to his *boyfriend* comment.

Twenty minutes passed before she heard another car outside. This time it was Cain. He entered the office and immediately smelled the cleaners she was employing.

"Wow, it smells very…" he paused, "antiseptic in here. It's been some time since this place was cleaned up. Thank you Ellie, but that really isn't an intern's job."

"Warden Cain, it's okay. I wanted to work in a clean environment and assumed you wouldn't mind that either. Oh, and Deke stopped by to give you this," she said as she handed him the plastic bag with the Glock inside. "You're supposed to call him too."

Warden Cain? he thought to himself. *I lost some ground in less than twelve hours…I better work on this relationship.* But time was not currently on his side. He looked at the Glock and he knew he had work to do.

Twenty minutes later Cain was chatting with Deke.

"So where exactly did you find it?"

"About thirty or forty feet from the main kill zone."

"We really didn't establish a main kill zone," Cain told him.

"Well I did. There is one area where the vegetation is extremely trampled and crush. It also is the area with the most blood and the blood spatter on the trees surrounds the area I reference. It was the main kill zone for at least two of the victims."

"How did the gun get so far away?"

"Holy shit, you're slow! Didn't you say the body parts were scattered everywhere? Why would the gun be any different?" Deke said in an exasperated raised voice.

"Yeah, you are right about that. Like you told Ellie, the magazine is empty, but it was definitely fired recently. So maybe we're looking for something wounded now."

"I doubt if it was wounded all that bad, Cain. It did a pretty thorough job on the victims and the dog. At least according to the report you emailed me. And if one of them was firing a pistol, he was probably the first to die. Predators usually eliminate threats in descending order if they are able."

Deke cleared his throat, but went silent.

"Deke, you are holding back. What's wrong?"

There was a long pause, "Cain, I know you think I like to make shit up sometimes. And I do like to weave a good yarn every now and again, but I found something pretty unusual."

"Pal, I trust you to tell me the truth. That's why I asked you to take a look. So give it to me."

"I found footprints. Not shoe prints. Not boot prints. Bonafide foot prints in the blood. I'm not surprised you missed them because I almost did. After I recognized a print I went looking for more. And lo and behold they were everywhere."

"Everywhere? We would have seen them. We're not incompetent, Deke. I assure you," Cain scolded.

"You guys were focused on the gore and the body parts and you walked all over the area like a battalion of infantrymen looking for a local beer joint. I'm not blaming you at all. You went in with the mindset for what seemed natural about this less than natural attack. But the prints I found were huge, which may be why you missed them. And something else that was pretty significant."

"Spit it out. This isn't one of your stories. Quit holding back and making me beg," Cain said angrily.

"It was bipedal. It walked upright, Cain. Like a man, but not a man."

It was now Cain's turn to go silent. He was trying to discern if Deke had lost it or not. His claim seemed preposterous.

"Why did you say *like a man, but not a man?*"

"The foot was deformed. The big toe was shifted too far to the left or right of the other toes. And the space between the big toe and the next toe was too deep. It was a foot, but it looked capable of some grabbing ability."

"Penelope and her monkey," Cain said as if in a trance.

"What does that mean?" the mountain man asked, confused.

"It means that the impossible may have become possible. Did you take pictures with that super clear camera of yours?"

"Yep. As soon as we hang up, I'll email them to you."

"Bye, Deke," he said cryptically.

He then sat waiting for the email to show up.

Chapter 9

Bad Moon Rising

A busy week passed. The Pennsylvania State Police Crime Lab sent Cain a ballistics report and analysis on the Glock that was found.

It was, in fact, the property of Ken McKenna. It was registered in his name, it was covered in his fingerprints and two spots of blood on the grip were a DNA match.

"So what was Ken shooting at?" the RAC said to Ellie. "What situation would have a man draw a deadly firearm, empty his magazine and then succumb to the very threat he was trying to stop?"

"Going by the information you have shared with me, an angry charging rhino," she said, not trying to be funny or cute.

"Oh no, Ellie," and he lowered his voice even though they were the only ones in the office. "This charging rhino, keep this to yourself, walked on two feet, according to Deke."

She added, "according to my research, the only animals in the State of Pennsylvania that could even remotely accomplish the things you say this one did are in zoos. I did more bear research too and ruled them out. Mountain lions couldn't do this either. Maybe Deke is on to something."

"Oh, come on, Ellie. Not you too. No one wants to say it, although I have to admit Doctor Slocum said so, that we might have us a bonafide Big Foot. And if I follow that trail I won't have my job next month."

"Didn't you get pictures from Deke?"

"Yep. Once you have the idea planted in your mind it does look like several large footprints. All hail the power of suggestion."

"Could I see them?" Ellie requested.

"Sure." He then spun his laptop around for her to see he had them on screen the entire time.

She stared with her mouth hanging open.

"Did you know what my favorite hobby is?" she asked him.

"No, but I'd love to."

"Cryptozoology."

"I've heard the term, but I am woefully ignorant as to what that really is."

"Warden Cain, it is the study of hidden animals."

"Meaning?"

"Dinosaurs, Big Foot, Yeti, Nessie, Chupacabra and so on."

It was Cain's turn to look slack jawed. He could feel his heart sinking. She was so pretty and smart and now he knew she was a nut. He started to resign himself to the fact that he was going to be a lifelong bachelor.

"I know what you are thinking, Jeremy Cain. No, I'm not a nut. It's a hobby, like fantasy football or a science like string theory. It is just for fun. It signifies that I wish there was still a little magic left in the world. Something unknown and discoverable. A small whiff of mystery to believe in," she explained.

"So you're really not a Big Foot believer?"

"No. After all this time something should have shown up to prove the existence of the mighty Sasquatch, but nope. Not a darn thing. But it's still fun to wonder why the Pacific coast Indian tribes believed in it. There has to be a grain of truth in there somewhere. Are you really that conservative that you don't dare dream beyond the known world?"

"Isn't the known world enough? Why look for monsters? We have bacteria that will eat you alive. Poisonous creatures by the dozens. And at least twenty-five active serial killers across the United States at any one time. Why look for more horrendous crap?"

"My ex-husband beat me once a week. While we were dating I never looked for monsters. We got married and I still didn't look for them. But guess what, Jeremy? The monster found me. Four months into the marriage Mr. Hyde showed up drunk.

"I put up with it for a short while and then I had him arrested. A restraining order was imposed. He violated it and violated me. I almost died. He is serving twenty years in prison. That monster has been catalogued and caged. So don't judge me for a little fantasy science to help explain the world. You see, I know horrendous crap first hand," she ended.

"I'm sorry, Ellie. Life sucks sometimes. I guess a bit of fantasy fun couldn't hurt," he apologized.

"If you're going to ask me out, don't let Big Foot stop you."

He smiled and shook his head. She was either this forward with everyone or she was reading him like a book. He decided to throw caution to the wind.

"Where would you like to go on our first date?"

"How about a picnic at Rothrock State Forest? Trailhead 3, to be exact. I would like to see things firsthand. I'll pack everything we need. You pick the day and time."

"Saturday. I'll pick you up at ten-thirty so we can be there before noon."

"It's a date."

State Game Land 118 wasn't far from Canoe Creek. On this day a four man logging team was assigned to clear out several areas of deadfall.

Clearing the accumulated fallen debris in the forest was a dangerous job at times. Kelly Houlihan, Toby Hardman, Tim Berky and Melron Washington were the best. They had the cleanest safety record and the highest efficiency rating of any of the eleven crews that did similar forestry clean up for the state. They were the hotshots of their profession.

State Game Land 118 would be host to deer hunters in less than a month. It hadn't been cleared out for years. The time for that was at hand.

Tim Berky hunted here as a boy. His family's roots were deep in this area. Whenever his team came back near to Canoe Creek, he felt like he was home. This time was no different.

His team always came prepared. The crew's equipment consisted of a dump truck, an industrial grade wood chipper called a wood hog and a large John Deere tractor with a grappler attachment for grabbing logs and a myriad of deadfall material. These large pieces of equipment were supplemented by the many chainsaws, limb saws and axes that were ever-present with the team.

Each member of the team also carried a personal firearm. Years of doing this work had taught them a valuable lesson: animals of every ilk loved to use deadfall areas as their home base. The men had more than once confronted mountain lions, bobcats, bears, warthogs, wolves (although strongly denied by state officials), coyotes and not a few angry, homeless human beings who had carved out a place within the piles of dead material.

Once they ousted a full grown tiger that had escaped from a local wildlife sanctuary. The tiger had been acquired and held illegally. When it escaped, the owners could not report it for fear of prosecution. The crew could not believe their eyes when the beautiful cat emerged from the thick pile of brush they were working to remove.

Luckily for them, the sound of their equipment kept the animal at bay. Special animal control agents were called in and the creature was captured and saved. The owners were caught based upon an anonymous tip after the story hit the media outlets.

That incident happened in the central part of the state close to the New York border. It was one of the crew's favorite stories to share when it was Miller time.

They had worked together for over fifteen years. Each man knew his assignment and each member looked out for the other. SGL 118 had seven large areas of detritus to be removed.

They had cleared two and were beginning on the third when the day ran out of sunlight. The temperature began to drop quickly. It would soon be Miller time. That was their code for happy hour.

Each man began the shut down required to maintain the heavy equipment. Locks were locked to make sure vandals or curiosity seekers didn't get themselves in a jam.

After the constant roar, whining and thrum of the various pieces of equipment, the silence of the forest was a welcome and sacred time for the crew. They relaxed and talked quietly.

Their comfort with one another had grown so great that no topic was off the table, religion and politics included. Melron was the only democrat/liberal of the group. Tim was middle of the road, leaving Kelly and Toby to fight hard for the conservative point of view.

After the recent contentious election, politics many times took center stage. The group made the arguments fun and although they were sometimes heated, they never crossed the line that would damage their friendships.

They argued religion the same way. Tim was a Protestant fundamentalist, Melron was a Baptist, and Kelly a Catholic. Toby was the lone atheist evolutionist.

All four men were college educated and their discussions were lively. It always surprised others that these modern day lumberjacks preferred to work out of doors rather than use their degrees to find employment that was much less physically challenging.

Tonight's debate found them all on the same side. Recent environmental issues going through the State House would possibly affect their jobs. Whenever environmental groups push their agendas, people lose jobs.

Their discussion came to a halt as they stood in the glow of a full moon. A shriek that sounded eerily like that of a woman pierced the night air.

Tim's reaction was to duck. It was that close. "What in the hell was that?" he asked.

Toby shrugged. Melron didn't answer and Kelly suggested, "let's get the hell out of here. Something doesn't feel right."

"Hey man, what's that smell?" asked Melron.

"Damn. Smells like a skunk crawled up a bear's ass and died," laughed Toby.

"What shrieks like that and then smells that bad?" Tim put out to the group.

Kelly repeated that they should go. He was extremely nervous.

"Calm down, Kelly. We're all armed, experienced woodsmen. Maybe we should check it out," suggested Melron.

"Seriously?" Tim posited. "You black guys always run from scary stuff. It's like in your bylaws or some shit."

"No, it's in our DNA. Lions and Tigers used to like to eat black people over there in the old country."

"Melron, I read that black people like to eat black people in the old country," Toby pipped in.

Tim couldn't resist. "Taste like chicken."

The three of them laughed, but Kelly wasn't having any of it. "Guys, I just saw something flitting between the trees. It was white."

"That figures," Melron said sarcastically.

"Look," Tim said as he pointed.

There, backlit by the trees, stood a figure standing next to the wood hog. All four men were rendered speechless and paralyzed as well.

It was upright on two legs and standing between seven and one half to eight feet tall. It was hairy, bowlegged and had tremendously long arms.

They heard a loud shriek only feet behind them. Kelly pissed himself as he turned to see the apparition of a woman with bulging eyes and open mouth. The other three men jumped and began reaching for their sidearms, never taking their eyes off the tall beast who had broken into a bounding run at the piercing sound which tore the night air asunder.

It was on Tim before his pistol could clear its holster. Tim became its weapon of choice as it used him as a bludgeon against Melron, knocking his gun out of his hands before he could fire a shot.

Toby began firing wildly at the creature, hitting Tim twice in the process. Tim's limp body then struck Toby full force, knocking him backwards. He retained his grip on his weapon.

Kelly stood staring at the woman as she shrieked a third time. He was never able to draw his weapon as fear had paralyzed him completely. He passed out where he stood. He would never regain consciousness.

Toby fired two more shots, missing, before the beast grabbed his arm and tore it from its socket. It then turned and clubbed Melron with it as he scrambled to find his weapon in the moonlight.

The beast dropped the arm and grabbed Melron by the head and twisted violently. He actually looked into the thing's eyes for the split second before his head separated from his body. It stared back as if he were some gruesome trophy.

The attack continued even after the four friends were dead. The shrieking woman stood by as the beast vented its rage upon the bodies of the four men.

Then as abruptly as it started, it ended. The full moon shone its beautiful light down upon the forest. The entire scene was bathed in a golden glow.

None of the woodland creatures dared to enter the kill zone. It was off limits. It was now tainted by hate, anger and death. The animals could see and feel the waves of corruption rising from that place. Man was clueless to the sensitive parts of life that the lesser mammals were in tune to.

Chapter 10

The Interruption

Cain hadn't been on a date in three years. He felt awkward as he picked Ellie up at her apartment in Meehan. She was ready with a small Igloo cooler and a Longaberger basket.

She got into the car before he could get out and open the door for her. As soon as she was seated and shut the door, he smelled the scents of heaven. First he discerned fried chicken and then a sweet coconut smell.

He had to swallow several times to keep from drooling on himself. And then he asked what he thought was a pertinent question, "Deke told me you can't cook. So whose handiwork am I smelling?"

"He caught me cleaning the office and asked me what I was doing, so I made stuff up. In other words, I lied. A woman likes to remain a mystery. I have other talents as well."

"Like what?" he asked.

"What part of *remain a mystery* didn't you understand?"

The date went on beautifully. They arrived at Rothrock and Jeremy insisted on eating their lunch in a picnic area. He told her that he could not eat anywhere near where the carnage took place.

The fried chicken was the best he had ever eaten. The sides included macaroni salad, baked beans and red beet eggs. The dessert was a coconut cake that almost sent Jeremy into a sugar coma. This was, without a doubt, the best meal he had eaten in years. A restaurant couldn't touch the taste or comfort value of this type of food.

The presentation was equally as impressive. Red and white gingham table cloth, matching napkins, plates with pictures of the Lochness Monster on one and Big Foot on the other. The serving spoons had dinosaur handles. This woman's sense of whimsy was endearing and Jeremy could feel his heart moving too quickly towards this engaging female.

After they had eaten, coaxed each other to burp aloud and packed everything into his SUV, they decided to walk to the trailhead. They needed to walk off some of the feast that they had just shared.

The forest was gorgeous and the air carried a hint of wood smoke from someone's campfire. The leaves were still putting on a show for anyone who cared to observe. Vibrant earth tones were always the prettiest palette as far as Ellie was concerned. She and Jeremy had that in common.

At the site of the attack, Ellie was first taken aback by how widespread the attack zone was. There were still many spots of blood on trees and vegetation. It hadn't rained in three weeks and very little evidence had been washed away.

Secondly, she was aghast at how violent the confrontation must have been. As Jeremy outlined the body part positions, she became overwhelmed with emotion. She began to cry softly.

When her date pointed to the places where the woman's breasts were found, the floodgates opened. She apologized and said she couldn't control her reaction.

Jeremy stepped forward and held her. He spoke gently, "could you cry some of those tears on my behalf? Being totally truthful, I wanted to cry that day, but with all the cops and other wardens around I had to hold it in. These were living, breathing human beings whose lives didn't deserve to end like this. It was horrific, sad and depressing. So cry Ellie. They deserve it."

She buried her face in his armpit. He loved the way this closeness felt, but he couldn't help but wonder how his deodorant was holding up.

She finally finished crying and looked him in the eye. "There's a human element at work here."

"Meaning?" he asked.

"I told you my hobby was cryptozoology, but we haven't discussed what my actual degree was in or why I am doing an internship in a Fish and Wildlife field office."

He faced her square on and said, "let's hear it."

"I have a Bachelor in Zoology from Cornell and I am getting my Master in Ethology from Franklin and Marshall."

"I am a bit of a dunce. What is ethology?"

"It is the study of animal behavior. And that is why I'm telling you there is a human drive behind these killings."

"Once again," he said pointing at his head, "dunce."

"What I mean is simple. No animal would have been driven to pull the woman's breasts off. That is a sadistic element for which only a human could take credit."

He was by no means an animal expert, but now that she pointed it out, he had been thinking that that element of the attack was extremely strange. Downright unnatural.

His phone rang. He pulled it from his pocket and checked the number. Pushing away from her he said, "sorry. I have to take this."

She could only hear his side of the conversation. "Cain here."

"Again. How many? Where?"

"All armed? Three? What about the fourth?"

"Yeah, I know that spot fairly well. I'll be there as fast as I can. Figure an hour."

He looked at Ellie. "There's been another attack. Game Land 118. We have to leave. I'll take you home first."

"No. Please take me with you. I can help. I have a camera in my purse if you need it."

"Ellie, you cried just hearing about it. Seeing it first hand is a whole new level of bad."

"Take me, Jeremy. Please?"

"Okay, Ellie. Don't embarrass me."

"I won't. And by the way, the footprints in the blood are not the power of suggestion at work. They are as plain as day to a cryptozoologist," and then she gave him an exaggerated toothy smile.

In spite of the current situation he laughed. It would be a long while before he laughed again.

One hour and seven minutes later they were pulling onto SGL 118. Another ten minutes on back roads brought them to a clearing with several large pieces of equipment.

There were also a warden's vehicle, belonging to Salas, three state police cruisers, a sheriff's cruiser, two ambulances and the medical examiners van.

Cain parked and got out of his vehicle. A lieutenant from the State Police walked over. "Hi. I'm Lieutenant Cox. I have been told to convey to you a message from Harrisburg. If you guys can't handle this situation the state will put together a task force and take care of it for you. Sorry for that, but I'm just the messenger."

"No problem, Lieutenant. Here's a message for Harrisburg. Tell them thank you. We could use all the help we can get."

"Seriously, Warden Cain? You know how vindictive those politicians can be. You might be short circuiting your career. They just want you to reassure them that you're on top of it."

"I am on top of it and I've got nothing. The only person to venture a guess refuses to be involved, which is just as well because he's way off base."

"What was his guess?"

"Lieutenant, he thinks it's Big Foot." Cain waited for a laugh or a look or any normal type of reaction.

The Lieutenant remained stone cold sober and said, "follow me."

By this time Ellie had gotten out of the car and was standing behind him out of the way. She heard everything and saw the trooper's reaction.

Cain turned to her, rolled his eyes and said, "come on. I have a sickening feeling we're going to get into your area of expertise."

They walked with the Lieutenant, passing by what appeared to be an arm lying in an area of short grass. A little ways farther the trooper stopped and turned, "Warden Cain, is your partner ready for the horror that these type of cases produce?"

"She says she is. She may be very helpful if you are going to show us footprints or any other unusual evidence."

"Ma'am, we are entering the epicenter of the kill zone. Please prepare yourself for the ugly side of life."

"I appreciate your concern, sir," she said, "but it's just meat."

The Lieutenant smiled.

Cain shook his head, raised his eyebrows and gawked at Ellie like she had two heads. He asked himself, *can this possibly be the woman I was holding in my arms less than two hours ago?*

Ellie noticed both of their reactions. The trooper thought he was being chivalrous, but came across condescending. And Cain asked her to be tough and not embarrass him. She promised him she wouldn't be a liability. In her mind she was being tough. She hoped Cain saw it that way.

The pieces and parts became more plentiful: a leg, two heads, a torso. The trooper stopped in an area of blood soaked sawdust.

"Look at those," he said while pointing.

There in the bloody sawdust were three very large footprints preserved in the morbid mixture.

Cain couldn't deny what he was seeing.

Ellie was in seventh heaven. The walk of horror to this evidence was worth it. What she observed was probably the greatest proof of a creature that has existed on the borders of scientific discovery.

The three prints were a cross between simian and human. The size was startling. The creature would have to be eight feet tall and weigh over five hundred pounds.

Because of her interest in cryptozoology, she had spent considerable time studying the similarities between man and ape. These three simple imprints needed to be preserved. She grabbed for her camera.

She also knew that these horrible circumstances would quickly knock down any claims of hoaxes and pranksters. The sacrifice of these victims would help to bring the claim of an alternative species to the forefront of the scientific community. And she would be the one to chronicle it.

She began snapping pictures and asking both Cain and the trooper if they had a plaster cast kit. The answer from both men was negative, but the Lieutenant said he would have two kits driven out to them.

Ellie asked Cain if he had a tape measure in the truck. He did and went to get it for her. When he returned, she set about measuring every aspect of the prints. She was in her element and it showed.

While she went about her business, the Lieutenant and Cain continued to walk the scene. Four torsos, four heads, eight arms and seven legs. Cain shared with the trooper that a leg was missing at each of the other two scenes. For now a logical answer for that coincidence remained a mystery.

Cain phoned Deke. "Hey, buddy, it happened again. A four man clearing crew over at SGL 118. It's bad, but I do have a question for you before you ask me any. Was that deer you photographed missing any of its limbs?"

"Yep. I couldn't find one of its legs. Some critter probably dragged it off. Why?"

"Deke, I'll call you later and explain everything."
He then hung up. It wasn't quite fair to Deke, but he needed
to do his job.

"Four pistols. Three unholstered and fired recently
and one that was never drawn," the Lieutenant shared.
They wrongfully assumed the owner of the holstered
weapon was the first killed.

A corporal walked up to his superior. "Sir, there are
two bullet wounds in one of the torsos. Neither would have
been fatal."

The scene kept becoming more bizarre. A large
clump of hair was found clutched in one of the dead hands.
To Cain's eye, it was the same kind of hair Slocum had
already identified as *great ape* hair.

Cain knew that he and Slocum were going to have a
face to face. It was necessary. The Big Foot connection was
becoming a real possibility, although Cain couldn't forget
what Ellie said about human involvement.

He wondered if Ellie could help him get Slocum to
help.

Chapter 11

An Ambush Of The Academic Kind

Cain had done all the research to find out Doctor Slocum's schedule. It wasn't all that difficult. A chatty lab assistant provided him with the times of his classes and where he enjoyed hanging out between them.

Slocum was a Starbucks fanatic. Ellie and Jeremy laid claim to a table near the back of the coffee shop facing the door. Cain had met the man twice. Both times he was working in an official capacity. He remembered quite well what Slocum looked like.

Doctor Slocum was rather unforgettable. He was short, balding and pudgy. Those attributes could be applied to millions, but what made the good doctor memorable was a harelip scar and Coke bottle glasses that made him look almost cartoonish. It was amazing that the responsibilities of his job required so much dependence on his eyesight.

Cain recognized him before he had even passed through the doorway completely.

"There he is," he told her. "Stay here."

Cain made his way over to the short line that was awaiting a barista's attention.

"Good morning, Doctor Slocum. Do you remember me?"

"Yes, Warden Cain. I was wondering how long it would be before you tracked me down."

Jeremy pointed to the table where Ellie sat with a beguiling smile playing across her face. "See that beautiful woman? She would like to meet you. You both have much in common."

"If she is a journalist, I have nothing to say."

"No, Doctor. She is just a lowly Fish and Game intern at my office in Canoe Creek. Her name is Ellen. She wants to share some information with you. No tricks."

The Doctor retrieved his coffee and joined them at their table. "Hello, young lady. I have less than twenty minutes to enjoy my coffee and you have less than that to convince me that you're interesting enough to talk to."

Ellie proceeded to slap down on the table several of the most clear shots of the footprints with an extended tape measure in the photo for scale.

Slocum picked them up. He held them fairly close to his face.

"What is making this ground appear so red?" he asked.

Cain let Ellie answer.

"That would be blood, Doctor. Lots of it mixed with sawdust and wood chips. The blood came from the creature's four victims."

Slocum looked quizzically at Ellie like he wasn't comprehending the words coming out of her mouth.

"You mean to say a Sasquatch attacked human beings so violently? And if that is so, was it with or without provocation?"

"Yes, and as far as we can tell, without provocation. This is the third attack in three weeks. So far a total of eight human beings and one dog. All torn apart. Literally dismembered," answered Cain.

"Bullshit. Sasquatch don't do that," declared Slocum.

"Why? Because they, as you put it, don't exist?" Cain shot back.

Ellie spoke. "Doctor, cryptozoology has been a hobby of mine for many years. This is the strongest evidence I have ever seen. And up to now what I have seen has been other people's findings. These are mine. First hand and shockingly convincing."

"Oh shit. It's happening all over again."

"Look Doc, I'll try to protect you on this, but we need someone with more knowledge than we have. And I don't even believe in this crap, but what I saw two days ago is working on my belief system something fierce."

"They do exist, Warden Cain, but most encounters have proven them to be shy, elusive and even gentle."

Ellie asked, "what about women who have claimed to have been kidnapped and raped by the beasts?"

"Oh my, you are just a hobbyist, aren't you?" Slocum chided. "You seem like a healthy young woman. I assume you have had a lover or two. Correct?"

Cain butted in. "Where in the hell is this going?"

Slocum ignored him. "Ellen, have you noticed taller men typically have longer, larger penises? It is an established corollary factor. Sasquatch males are said to be in the eight foot height range and weighing five hundred pounds. Are you getting my drift?"

She blushed a dark red and answered, "mating with a Sasquatch would be a painful, singular event. Even if you survived it."

"What does that mean?" Cain asked a little miffed that Slocum had continued his questions with Ellie.

"Jeremy, it means, all things being proportional, Sasquatch would probably kill a human woman if he mated with her," Ellie explained with some embarrassment.

"Unless the beast is more similar to a lowland gorilla, which only has an erect penis length of one and a half to two inches. But all other physiological indicators seem to rule that out," the doctor concluded.

"So penises aside, will you help us?" Cain pleaded.

"Yes, Warden Cain, but my name stays out of it unless there is a real scientific discovery."

Cain and Ellie answered at the same time. "Deal."

"Well, my time is up. I need to return to class. When may we meet so that I may be brought up to speed on these current events?"

"You name it," Cain offered. "We'll work around your schedule."

A time was set to meet and the doctor left.

Jeremy and Ellie headed back to the office.

An hour later they parked in the office parking lot next to Deke's pickup. Cain had given Deke a key two years ago.

They walked in and Cain began, "so, mountain man, what brings you out into civilization today?"

"Holy shit, Cain, pardon my French, Ellie. I think I might have some interesting thoughts regarding your attacks. That is, if you two are done running around instead of working."

"We were working, Deke. We were enlisting the aid of an expert," Ellie said as Jeremy shot her a dirty look. She had forgotten Slocum wanted no mention of his name. After she caught Jeremy's look she remembered quickly.

"What expert are you referring to, Ellie? An expert in murder in the woods? Because I think that is what you got. Plain and simple," Deke informed them.

"Our expert is anonymous at this juncture. And what do you mean by murder?" Cain asked.

"I mean Penelope is killing those people as revenge."

"The dead witchy woman?" Cain asked incredulously.

"Now dammit, Cain, don't give me that look like I'm a crazy Grizzly Adams wannabe who's lost his mind."

"Well, aren't you a crazy Grizzly Adams wannabe?"

"Yeah, but I haven't lost my mind."

"Sounds like it to me. How about you Ellie? Do think he's lost his mind?"

She looked at Cain and winked. "I think he sounds bat shit crazy. But I would like to hear his theory. I'm sure it's entertaining."

"Very funny. Are you two done with your Stiller and Meara routine? I have a very plausible line of thinking."

"Okay, Deke. Ellie and I are all ears."

"What year is this?"

"2017," answered Ellie.

"And Cain this is for you. What year did I tell you Penelope was killed?"

"1817," Jeremy answered.

"Exactly two hundred years, right? Exactly."

"Deke, no more questions. Get to your point."

"Each attack included a descendant from the original gene pool from the town known as Canoe Creek.

All them other people and the dog were just in the wrong place at the wrong time, with the wrong person. She's exacting her revenge on the two hundredth anniversary of her death," Deke explained.

"Why two hundred years, Deke? What's so significant about that?" Ellie queried.

"Hell, I don't know. Maybe there's a statute of limitations in the spirit world. Like maybe no revenge after two hundred years or something," Deke said exasperated because he knew how stupid it sounded.

Deke pressed on. "Look, Cain. Think about it. Three of those victims were originally from Canoe Creek or rather their ancestors were. The whole damn town back in the early 1800's could only boast about eighty-five people."

"Deke, you got this crap from a book, right?" asked Cain. "Did they name anyone? The accusers or the men who supposedly dispatched the woman?"

"Geez, Louise. Don't call it dispatched. She was murdered. This is more serious than you think."

"Deke, contact the author of the book. See if he or she has any names. At least then you could start to build a case, but for now nobody is going to believe anything about a witch when we have hair samples and foot prints. Everything points to an animal."

"You're right, Cain, but this animal is acting beyond peculiar, don't you think? And your animal is unbelievable as my witch. We're talking dead people here, buddy. Don't rule out anything."

"Get those names, Deke and I'll feel better about your idea. Until then, it's too far-fetched," Cain said softly. He could see Deke was agitated and embarrassed.

"I'm leaving. This isn't going to stop, *Ranger*. It's not," Deke said as he headed towards the door.

Cain yelled, "quit calling me *Ranger!*"

"Screw you!" And then he was out the door and in his truck. He peeled out, leaving those behind with the message that he was pissed.

Chapter 12

And Yet More

The throaty sounds of racing four wheel ATVs filled the air. The two sets of brothers had taken to meeting every weekend in the fall to ride their machines among the muddy tracks and hills of the Rothrock State Forest.

The four men were in a conservation area that was meant to be off limits to off-road vehicles. They knew, as everyone did, that there were not enough wardens to cover such an expansive area. And if they did get caught, all they would receive is a slap on the wrist.

Riding was what they lived for. Each one wore a distinctive jumpsuit, matching helmet and reflectorized goggles. They all rode on the amateur sprint circuit in western Pennsylvania.

Four-wheel ATV racing was considered by many to be the most dangerous of all the racing sports. Almost every race had one major injury to its credit. Sometimes two and the crowd ate it up.

There were also occasional fatalities, after which attendance would increase for the next few races. ATV racing was considered a blood sport. It was the nature of the beast and the riders and the crowds were thrill seekers.

Today was a typical practice day for the group. Tearing around the hills and torn up tracks that dirt bikes had made helped to hone their skills. This terrain was far worse than the racing courses they faced.

The sun was beginning to set as they gathered at the pickups with their trailers waiting to haul their rides home.

Mike Feathers, the oldest, had brought a case of Yuengling Lager. The reward after a hard workout.

As they dusted themselves off and removed their gear, they began the banter that had become so easy between them. Mike's brother, Todd, was dating a college girl from Ohio who was attending Penn State. That was worth weeks of telling Todd she was too smart for him. Once they found a subject, they usually beat it to death. Todd just developed a thick skin.

Randy and Jim Littman were the other brothers. They both were community college graduates. The brothers were bright, but not very motivated to go out and find good paying jobs. That would cut into their ATV playtime.

The beer was providing the four with a relaxing respite before heading back home. Although they drank often, they never seemed to get drunk. Their beer time just took the edge off of the day and gave them an excuse to enjoy each others company.

That enjoyment, this particular evening, was shattered by a shriek off to the west, but close by.

"What the hell was that?" asked Mike.

No one answered. The other three stood motionless and looking fairly concerned. After about a minute, Todd went to the cab of Mike's truck and pulled out a Cimarron 1875 Outlaw Colt 45. It was his pride and joy.

He bought it because it reminded him of the old John Wayne westerns he watched with his dad. The other men admired it as well. It was a beautiful firearm.

"What do you think you're going to do with that?" Randy asked nervously.

"I don't know about you guys," Todd said, "but when that thing, whatever it is, screamed, I almost shit my pants!"

Randy agreed. "Yeah, I got a bad feeling too. Do you have any more guns in the cab?"

Mike spoke up. "Just so happens that I do."

Mike went to his cab and removed two twin Mossberg Model 500 Classic 12 gauge pump action shotguns.

"Just bought these off a buddy who needed money real bad. Like new, two hundred and fifty dollars each."

He handed one to Randy with some shells and kept one for himself.

"What about you, Jimmy? What are you going to use?" Todd asked.

Jimmy was the quietest of the four, but when he spoke he usually brought down the house.

"Well, Todd. The way I see it, I'm using three red neck assholes with shotguns and a six shooter. And if they don't shoot each other, I'll feel safe enough. Plus I got this."

He bent over and pulled up his pant leg. And with one lightning fast motion he stood before them holding a Cold Steel boot knife.

As they began to laugh, their levity was cut short by another shriek. This was much closer. All four felt like shitting their pants.

Their bravado depleted and they began to back up toward the trucks. They couldn't leave yet. The ATVs weren't loaded onto the trailers.

The creature stared at its victims from forty feet away. It felt the danger that it faced. They held things that it knew could cause it harm. It wished she would just let them go. This wasn't a fight it wanted to be a part of.

Then it saw the woman that controls, that makes the noise. She was staring at the men too. Waiting. Then she turned and looked at the beast. The creature was terrified and knew what was coming. The anger and the hatred and the hunger. Part of one of those men was going to be its next meal. But it wouldn't remember a thing until it was time to find the best piece of meat to eat so it could regain its strength. It would see the carnage and reason that it had caused it, but would not remember the actual actions that it took.

"Look," Mike said, "I just saw, what looked like, a woman in a white gown running between the trees."

"No regular ol' woman made that noise, bro," Todd argued.

"Remember them hikers a few weeks back?" Randy asked.

"Yeah the ones with the girl that lived, but was totally messed up saying she saw a monkey or some shit. I heard she's at the Beacon House with the other loons," Jim chirped in. "I heard she's still there and still bat shit crazy."

A shriek pierced the night so close to them they all jumped.

"Over there!" Mike yelled in a high pitch that gave away his level of fear to the others. There wasn't one among them ready to give him a hard time. They were all in the panic zone.

The other three men looked to where Mike pointed.

It was just thirty feet away and huge. It broke towards them and covered the open ground between them in seconds. But it wasn't quite fast enough.

Mike leveled his shotgun and fired.

The thing roared.

Todd's Colt fired two shots before Randy's shotgun spouted and ended Todd's life.

Jim dropped his knife and ran.

All hell broke loose upon that little patch of open land.

The shrieks continued as the beast did its deed.

Four days had passed since Deke's angry departure. Cain was getting a little worried. He had called his friend three times and left messages apologizing. Ellie had joined him on one of the messages hoping that acting cutesy would win him over enough for a return call. No luck.

Cain and Ellie sat in the office talking about a series of memorandums that had just been handed down from the state. The gist of the memos was that quarterly reports were soon due and some wardens were getting lackadaisical about accuracy.

They both heard an engine outside roar into a parking spot and go quiet. The next sound was the squeak of a door. One minute later Deke was in the office pouring himself a cup of coffee.

"Well, what the hell are you two staring at?"

Cain smiled. "Deke, we thought you were mad at us."

"No. I'm mad at you, not this pretty fawn sharing your office."

"She's a little older than a fawn, Deke," Cain quipped.

"Okay. Now I'm angry with you too, Warden Cain. I could still be a fawn if I wanted to be."

"Anger aside, what brings you back to our little patch of heaven, Deke? More ghosts? Bigger Bigfoots? What?"

"Are you sassin' me, boy? I'm here to help you. And who said anything about Bigfoot?"

"Have a seat my friend. There are some things I need to tell you." Cain explained the mounting evidence pointing towards what most people would describe as an impossibility.

When Cain was finished, Deke had some questions. "You mean to tell me that some candy-ass scientist over at the college thinks we got ourselves a genuine Bigfoot? And he wants to remain anonymous? If I came up with that shit, I'd want to be anonymous too."

Cain couldn't wait to point out the obvious. "Deke, you think it's the ghost of a woman who has been dead for two hundred years. How can you possibly have trouble with a Bigfoot, especially since we have footprints and hair to back it up?"

"Because Bigfoot doesn't exist and ghosts do. Them paranormal people have their own TV shows now. They've got pictures and everything. Hell, I've got a picture of Penelope from my trail cam. But no one has anything credible on a Bigfoot."

Ellie couldn't help herself. She started giggling and couldn't stop.

Deke turned towards her. "Which one of us are you laughing at? The crazy Bigfoot theorist or the sensible ghost whisperer?"

The question made her lose it even more. She was turning red and began to cough, literally laughing so hard she was choking.

Cain jumped up and got her a cup of tap water.

"Here, Ellie. I don't want you to die here and then haunt me for the rest of my life. You know, because ghosts exist and Bigfoot doesn't," Cain joked, which sent Ellie darn near into convulsions.

Deke just rolled his eyes and shook his head.

This comedic tour de force would have continued, but the phone rang. Ellie was in no condition to answer it, so Cain took the call. His expression changed immediately and a black cloud crossed his brow.

Ellie's laughter ended abruptly when she saw Cain's expression. Deke knew the call was bad as well.

When Cain hung up the phone, he said, "that was the State Police. It happened again. A group of ATV enthusiasts were slaughtered. Two young boys on dirt bikes found them this morning. Ellie, call Salas and Sorenson. Have them meet me at Rothrock Conservation Area 7." He turned to Deke and said, "up for a ride?"

Deke put his hand on Cain's shoulder and said, "sonny boy, you couldn't keep me away."

Chapter 13

A Piece Of The Beast

Pulling into Conservation Area 7, Cain could feel the doom and gloom descending upon him. Three state cars were parked behind two pickups with empty trailers.

Three ATVs were parked at the end of those trailers and one ATV was lying in the back of one the trucks upside down. The truck's cab was partially stoved in. It looked as if the ATV was thrown, hit the top of the cab and then fell back into the bed of the   truck.

Deke had the exact same impression. "Cain, what the hell could throw an ATV like that?"

"Has to be another explanation, Deke, but I admit I'm thinking the same thing. Like something that strong could tear a person limb from limb. Holy shit."

"When did you start swearing, Cain?"

"I started when my forests became a slaughterhouse for some unknown creature."

"You mean ghost, and we know who she is."

"Don't start with me, Deke. I don't need that crap right now. We need to follow the clues before the State Police decide to take over and turn everything to shit."

They saw a state policeman walking their way. It was Lieutenant Cox. Same guy that told him his time was limited before he lost jurisdiction.

"Hey fellas. So we meet again, Warden Cain. Things don't seem to be getting any better. Have you figured out what type of animal is doing this?"

Deke spoke up. "It ain't no animal. It's a ghost."

Cox stepped back with a smile on his face. "What?"

Cain interjected quickly. "Don't listen to him Lieutenant. He's my simple minded uncle and this is my day to watch him." Then Cain reached over quickly and grabbed Deke's arm hard to shut him up.

Cain continued, "we have a wildlife expert from Penn State looking at the clues. He says he is zeroing in on what it might be."

"He better be fast, Cain, because whatever or whoever did this went up against yet another group of men who were armed to the teeth. And they too fired their weapons, shotguns and a revolver. And we have a chunk of material your animal expert can look at. It appears that one shotgun blast hit one of their own, so we know they were panicked. But another blast hit its mark."

Cain could hear Deke saying under his breath, "Simple minded damn uncle. Asshole."

Cox walked away and Cain looked at Deke. "What in the hell is wrong with you? Did you not get how important this is? The Pennsylvania State Police may swoop in and try to take over. And if you keep spouting off about ghosts, that will damn sure guarantee they will do it sooner than later, Uncle Deke."

"I ain't your damn uncle. I'll be quiet, but don't tell no one else that I'm simple minded. Got it!"

"Got it. Now let's get out of this truck and figure out what the hell is going on. Sounds like we have a piece of the animal to look at. Maybe it's something we can recognize."

Two troopers were standing over an area where three limbs were resting. All three were legs belonging to the ATV victims. Next to those limbs was what looked like a piece of matted fur that was approximately eight inches by five or six inches.

Cain bent down to examine it. He turned it over with his ballpoint pen. A healthy chunk of flesh was attached to the fur and he could make out two pieces of buckshot clinging to the meat.

It was a close in shot, but obviously not enough to stop the animal's rampage. Cain looked over at Deke whose mouth was hanging slack. He really did look simple minded.

"Now does that look like a damn ghost to you, Deke? This is a mammal of some kind. And if stench were the only indicator, then I'd say we're dealing with a monster skunk. Damn that thing stinks!" He paused to swallow and control his gorge. "Hell, even a skunk doesn't smell that bad."

Deke whispered, "you know, Cain. I have read some accounts of people who said they had encountered Bigfoot and many of them have noted the terrible stench that comes from the damn thing. Maybe you're onto something."

"Keep whispering my friend, because the State Police aren't going to buy that any more than they were going to believe your ghost theory. We're on our own with this."

Salas and Sorenson showed up twenty or so minutes later. Both had come from separate directions but had arrived simultaneously. They found Cain and Deke touring the horrendous scene of human tragedy.

"What do we have, sir?" Sorenson asked.

"We have four heads, four torsos, eight arms and seven legs, along with two trucks, two trailers, four ATVs, two shotguns and a Colt .45 revolver. All recently fired. We have one chunk of an animal we can't identify. And one hell of a big problem. Does that about cover it, Deke?"

Deke shook his head. "That covers it except the part about something picking up one of the ATVs and throwing it into the back of that truck over there."

The two newly arrived wardens looked to where Deke was pointing.

"Holy shit!" Salas exclaimed. "What could do that?"

"We don't know," Cain said. "Keep your weapons loaded and ready at all times out here. In fact, grab your shotguns. We can't take any chances."

Salas and Sorenson returned to their vehicles and grabbed their shotguns and loaded them. They were watching each other as they did it. Both were shaking their heads. Both were scared.

The medical examiner gave his best guess as to time of death for Cain and Cox. Cause of death was a no-brainer.

Cox said, "I have to get back on the road. My two guys will stay until you're finished bagging and tagging, but Cain, I ordered them to be out of here before dark. I would suggest you do the same."

Cain, Deke and the wardens joined the ambulance crew, the two troopers and the coroner's men who were trying to wrap this up. A convoy of tow trucks and a flatbed was arriving to take care of all the vehicles assembled at the scene.

Three miles away the creature lay on its side in a patch of ferns. The bleeding hadn't yet subsided. It moaned piteously. The shotgun blast had torn away a chunk of flesh from its hip. Quite a few pieces of buckshot were embedded in the beast. It had never felt such pain before in its life.

It had been right to be concerned about those things the weak smooth creatures carried in their hands. It also had been grazed in the shoulder by a .45 caliber bullet, but that was nothing. The hip wound was the injury that had it most fearful.

The hunger had come and gone, just like before, despite its injuries. It had feasted on Todd's leg. It didn't enjoy its food. The hunger was an uncontrollable force to be sated by the flesh of its victims. It was never a pleasurable experience.

It would lay in the ferns for a while. It needed its energy to heal. Moving hurt too much. It closed its eyes and slept fitfully.

They finished with about an hour and a half of daylight to spare. All parts and pieces had been collected. Cain would bring Deke and Ellie out here again tomorrow. He had noticed two areas that appeared to have tracks similar to the last site.

He wanted Ellie to make some castings to be sure and he wanted Slocum to look at his latest prize. He also wanted him to see the scene of the attack. Once Slocum saw the horror close-up, he had to become more interested.

Cain had Ellie call to make the arrangements. Tomorrow would come soon enough. He was emotionally depleted. He had to get to the bottom of this situation and fix it.

Until then Rothrock was closed to the public. Harrisburg was sending additional wardens to work under Cain. They wanted results. The shit storm had just begun.

The State Police were also mulling over what to do, but with the chunk of the beast having been found, it was clearly out of their domain. No crime had been committed other than trespassing on conservation land. And it was still labeled as an animal attack.

Upon returning to the office, Cain walked in to find that Ellie had somehow replicated their picnic that had been interrupted. She had made provision for Deke too.

The smell of fried chicken filled the room. There was a huge chocolate cake waiting to be eaten as well. After the stench of that creature, this was truly heaven on earth.

Deke kept trying to make excuses to leave them alone and Ellie wouldn't hear of it. "Deke, you were out there all day too. How often do you get to eat a home cooked meal?"

"Never, actually," he replied.

"When did you have time to do all this if you were here?" Cain asked with a little awe in his voice.

"I wasn't here. I read the phone manual and figured how to forward calls to my cellphone. So I could cook and work at the same time. For the record, I didn't leave until 3:30 pm. I monitored you guys with the extra walkie talkie and tried to time everything just right. How did I do?"

Deke laughed. "Miss Ellie, if he don't marry you, I'd like to."

"I'll keep that in mind, Deke," she giggled.

She then filled the guys in on her day and phone calls while they ate. They did the same for her.

They all laughed heartily when she exclaimed, "you're kidding? Your simple minded uncle?"

Chapter 14

Slocum, Ellie And Deke

The SUV filled with four passengers drove into Rothrock to continue their investigation. Ellie had brought plenty of plaster to make molds per Cain's request. Slocum, after seeing the large chunk of the animal's flesh, began to show some real interest. Especially after he smelled the thing. He would look for any additional evidence and try to understand as much as he could from the scene of the attack.

Cain and Deke were there to provide security. Both were armed with 10 gauge pump action shotguns. They weren't taking any chances.

On the drive over, Slocum was very chatty. "Did you know that many people who claim to have seen the animal up close and personal have complained of its unnaturally foul odor? I believe it is caused by scent glands that secrete the odor so that the creatures can find each other.

"You see, people like to romanticize the Bigfoot legend. They think the things live in families or colonies because we live in families and colonies. I say, *rubbish*. I believe they are solitary creatures which is how they have remained so elusive. Groups would draw attention to themselves.

"A group of the things would leave areas broken down and depleted. Much in the same way that man destroys his environment in his day to day existence. And mind you, these things are huge."

Deke was seated in the backseat with Ellie. He leaned forward. "Did that chunk of meat and hair convince you that they exist?"

"Sir, I have always believed they existed. I just couldn't say so. Admitting your belief on this subject is akin to yelling fire in a crowded movie house. Once you can't prove there was a fire, then everyone hates and distrusts you. That is what its like for Bigfoot hunters and believers.

"They make Discovery and Animal Planet specials from the kooks on the fringe. It's entertaining to see grown men and women swear there is a monster and not be able to prove it."

"So that piece of mammal was definitely Sasquatch?" Cain asked.

"Yes, Warden Cain. You bet your sweet ass that was a Sasquatch. That was the best piece of proof I've ever seen and I've seen plenty. Over the years I've examined teeth, bones, hair, footprints and scat. I was even brought a mummified paw, but that turned out to belong to a large orangutan.

"But what you brought me is being DNA sequenced as we speak. I already examined the fur. Like nothing I've seen since I was on the West Coast."

They pulled into Conservation Area 7. All conversation ceased. The four exited the vehicle. The area was defined by yellow tape with the words *Police Line Do Not Cross* printed on it.

Slocum couldn't believe how large an area was involved. He looked around and very quickly began to spot areas awash with crimson. He began trying to calculate how much blood four average size human males would yield. He settled on five and a half to six gallons.

"Doctor, as you can see, you have a rather large area to look for clues. And Ellie, come with me. There are two areas that looked good yesterday for a plaster cast of the footprints."

They all set about doing their work. Cain helped Ellie with the plaster. Deke walked a perimeter around the group holding tight to his 10 gauge. He would never admit it to the others, but this whole affair had him unnerved. He had an additional reason to be worried. He would keep it to himself.

"Hey, over here!" Doctor Slocum yelled. "I think I found something."

They all hurried over to where he was.

"Look," he said, pointing to the ground.

There in a patch of damp ground were the footprints of a child or small woman. To Ellie they contrasted greatly to the plaster casts her and Jeremy had just finished. But why were they here?

Deke looked at Cain and said, "meet Penelope."

"I thought you said she was a ghost, Deke. Ghosts don't leave footprints."

"Well hell, Ranger. They don't pose for photographs either, but she did."

"If you're right, why would she be hanging around Bigfoot? And stop calling me *Ranger*."

Slocum looked at the other three. "Who the hell is Penelope?"

Cain and Ellie turned to Deke. This was his part of the show. Deke went into his story. He included the trail cam evidence, if you could call it that, and he concluded with the lone survivor's litany which she had repeated over and over, *Penelope and her monkey*.

"Wow. I thought believing in Bigfoot was a stretch, but a pissed off witch is a whole new paradigm. And a pissed off witch who has befriended Bigfoot is beyond my grasp. Truly," Slocum declared.

"Well, what if she didn't befriend him?" Deke put forth.

"Meaning?' Slocum asked.

"What if she is using him? After all, you're the one who said violent behavior isn't part of the behavioral pattern of these things. At least that's what Cain said that you said."

"I did say that. But Mr. Humboldt, your witch theory is a wild theory. You have to admit that."

"Doc, the first time someone approached you about Bigfoot, did you find that a bit of a stretch too?"

"Yes, Mr. Humboldt, but a new species with a little evidence is easier to handle. New species are found all the time. Witchcraft and ghosts are still marginalized by the scientific community. They are Halloween legends and no more."

Deke walked away shaking his head and could be heard saying under his breath, but loud enough to be heard, "educated prick. Doesn't know shit from shinola."

"Sorry, Doctor Slocum. He's a passionate man and he really believes he has hit on something here. He even has a theory about each attack involving descendants involved in Penelope's murder."

"Any of these guys fall into that category?"

"I know the name *Feathers* has been a name that seems to be ingrained in this area. It wouldn't surprise me if the bloodline harkens back to the early eighteen hundreds," Cain explained.

"Any theories on why all this is happening now?" the doctor inquired.

"Only Deke's theory," Ellie offered up. "He thinks it's revenge."

They got quiet as Ellie photographed the small footprints. Cain looked for Deke and located him over by the SUV smoking a cigar. Cigars were Deke's emotional pacifier. He didn't smoke often, but when he was upset, the rolled tobacco soothed his nerves.

The beast began to stir. It smelled smoke. Three miles away it could detect Deke's cigar and know that it wasn't a wood fire. That's the only kind of fire it worried about. Forest fires had claimed its kind before.

It pushed itself up. The pain was excruciating. The blood loss had stopped, but it was definitely weakened. Flies had covered the wound. It didn't care. It laid back down, too tired to look for food.

The beast had a passing thought of the screaming woman and shuddered. It hoped she wouldn't show up again. It always hoped that, but as of yet that wish hadn't been granted.

It moaned itself back to sleep.

The group loaded into Cain's vehicle and began the drive back to State College to drop the doctor off. After which they would return to the office.

Deke was grumpy and quiet. Doctor Slocum was occupied writing onto his iPad that he had brought with him. The only conversation was between Jeremy, Ellie and eventually Deke.

"When we get back to the office, we can eat leftover chicken if you like. There is plenty for the three of us," she offered.

"Sounds good, Ellie, but I don't know if Grumpy back there will be hungry," Cain said referring to Deke.

"Dammit, Ranger. What do I got to do to make you people believe what I'm telling you? That woman is out there! She keeps killing and if you don't acknowledge her part in this, it's not going to stop. Those Feathers boys belong to a family that has been here since the beginning of the settlement of this area back in the early nineteenth century."

"That's what I told the doctor there. Your theory could hold water, Deke. How do we prove it?" asked Cain. "And stop calling me *Ranger!*"

"You got the footprints. There's no other explanation for them."

"We'll talk about it some more if you eat chicken with us. How about that?" Cain said.

"Screw your chicken. I need a drink."

Truth be told, Cain had the same idea. They all needed to unwind. Maybe he'd pick up a cold six pack on the way back.

Ellie read his mind. "Do you want to stop for a couple cold ones to have with the chicken?"

"Yes, I do."

Twenty minutes later they dropped Doctor Slocum in front of his condo. He had something to say before he left them.

"Folks, I still want to remain anonymous as far as this venture is concerned. I do believe you are onto something real and exciting. And from what you showed me, extremely dangerous. With that said, I will let you know what the DNA sequencing reveals.

"I will be amassing incontrovertible evidence before I am willing to step forward out of the shadows. Until then I would advise that you tread lightly as well, on both the Bigfoot and witch front. Neither will sell well. I have been through that humiliation before. Talk to you soon."

As they drove off, Deke said to no one in particular, "windbag pussy know-it-all."

"So you like the doctor then," joked Ellie.

"No, I do not! He's ready to get all doe-eyed about Bigfoot, but my witch is a stretch for him. Cut me a break."

Cain looked in the rearview mirror. "Deke, we have a piece of an unknown creature, but only a strange photo of the witch, as you call her. We all just need more proof for both. Okay?"

"I'll get you your damn proof," and then Deke clammed up.

The rest of the ride was in silence. Even when Cain jumped out to grab a six pack, Deke didn't utter a word to Ellie as they sat alone in the vehicle.

At the office Deke grunted a goodbye and jumped into his truck and drove off.

"Poor man," Ellie observed.

"Yeah, his feelings are hurt. I've seen him like this a couple of times before. When he says he'll find proof, he just might. Knowing him, he'll double down until he finds something credible to offer up."

"He won't do anything foolish, will he?" she asked.

Cain smile. "Ellie, we're talking Deke. Foolish is right in his wheelhouse."

They went into the office and enjoyed the chicken, beer and pleasant conversation. They put the day's events out of their heads as evening approached.

Deke, however, was just getting started.

Chapter 15

Deke

Deke set up his cellphone on a flexible jointed tripod on the kitchen counter. The camera faced the little kitchen table where he ate his breakfast every morning.

On the table itself were several books on the occult and several piles of handwritten notes and computer generated printouts. In these moments, this was his war room.

He turned the camera app to record and then sat down in the well-worn kitchen chair that had been his favorite for many years. The other three chairs at the table showed very little wear. Deke did not often have guests in his small log cabin home.

Cain was Deke's closest friend. Everyone else treated him as either an oddity or outright lunatic. He was a man in tune with nature and all things natural. His one concession to the modern world was technology in the form of his cellphone and his computers.

He shunned television and owned one that was twenty-five years old. A nineteen inch Sony from the large picture tube days. It had plenty of life left in it because it was rarely on. Deke's major television concessions were NFL football and Swamp People on the History Channel. Outside of that programming, the TV just sat collecting dust.

He was an avid reader about all things wild and wooly. He was also interested in the occult. He never did anything unseemly, but he liked to read about it. He found the spirit world and magic fascinating.

It was that fascination which led him to read about local area legends including Penelope and her ruined wedding day. Even before the trail cam photo, Penelope's story had captivated him.

Deke had a backstory that most people wouldn't dare to imagine. He had left a woman standing at the altar when he was twenty-seven years old.

There was no soap opera story to go with the event. He simply had gotten cold feet. The woman, Katherine, had their life together all mapped out. She was going to be a successful dentist and Deke was going to be an up and coming lawyer. That is another fact that only a few people knew about him.

Deke was a Harvard Law graduate. Magna cum laude to be more specific. Deke loved the learning, but the application seemed to be an endless stream of whom could out-bullshit whom.

Suits and ties made him as uncomfortable as standing next to a buzzing beehive. He hated the formality and the one-upmanship of corporate fashion. It wasn't a life that he could embrace.

Poor Katherine stood at the church, being consoled by almost everyone. Deke sat on the end of an old fishing pier, fishing in a tuxedo. Several other people fishing along the banks nearby stared in disbelief, but no one cared to inquire about any details.

Penelope's wedding interruptus brought his own story flooding back. He felt heartily sorry for Katherine and the humiliation she suffered. After reading about Penelope, he thought to himself, *at least Katherine wasn't dragged out of the church andmurdered.*

Deke practiced law for two years more and then quit. He made enough to buy his little cabin next to a babbling brook filled with trout. He then did some consulting work for small businesses and hired himself out as a hunting and fishing guide. Eventually the guide work was all he did.

His crazy woodsman persona was birthed once his hair reached his shoulders and his beard hung down from his chin seven or eight inches. People loved to judge others by their looks. He used it to his advantage. Everyone wanted a guide that looked like John the Baptist in the wilderness.

He didn't miss female companionship too often. Once in a while he would visit a young woman in a nearby trailer park. She was happy to let him contribute to her children's college fund, as she put it, in exchange for some feigned intimacy.

On the whole, Deke was a happy man. He faced life on his own terms. And now he felt a need to prove himself to his friends Jeremy Cain and Miss Ellie. He felt he was onto something with the Penelope aspect of the current situation. He just had to make his case.

As the camera app recorded, he began.

"Ranger," he smiled directly into the camera. "Miss Ellie, I aim to prove my theory. Let me start with this. It's an old axiom from England and then the colonies.

Good witch ere a dead witch
On this count tis true
Unless she return
On century two
Old lines of blood

No revenge will delay
The spawn of her killers
All debt must pay

"If you haven't picked up on it, this is what it says. Dead witches are the best witches until they have been dead for two hundred years. At that time, they are allowed, by whom I do not know, God I guess, to return and get revenge against the descendants of their original slayers.

"I found that in a book called, Good Witch, Dead Witch by Emanuel Nathans. It was a compendium of witch lore and history. Great read, by the way.

"This is Penelope's two hundredth year. Those men from the church killed her and she's getting her revenge against the bloodline. She seems to be sticking to the forests for some reason. I don't have an explanation for that. But that's a good thing. We wouldn't want her making house calls, now would we?"

He stood up and turned the camera app off. Tonight he would drink to summon his courage. Tomorrow night he would be staying at the first attack sight where the hikers and their dog died. He knew it would be a dangerous venture, but he was looking for a thrill or two.

Cain picked Ellie up at her place. They were headed to State College to go out for dinner and a movie. The bond between them was growing.

She had never been to Baby's Burgers. It was a little like Johnny Rockets, in that it was a throwback to the fifties and sixties. The food was delicious and the thick shakes could make an ice cream lover cry tears of joy. The perfect date eatery.

The movie was the latest installment of the Johnny Depp pirate movies. Cain didn't care for them much, but Ellie was a big fan. As long as Ellie had a good time, then all was good.

Ellie felt the same way. She wanted Cain to be happy with their time together. Although she was under no obligation, she wanted Cain to know she had a child. A little four year old boy who was currently living with his grandparents. Her ex-husband's parents to be more specific. The ex was still living.

The man was serving forty years for voluntary manslaughter. She had divorced him when their son was only a year old. She found being a single mother to be overwhelming while going to school and her ex-husband's parents all but begged her to let them help.

Some people called that being a bad mom, but she was trying to better herself so she could be a great mom and support them both. She wasn't sure how Cain would feel about it. She wanted to bank as many good experiences as possible so that Cain would see what a good woman she was and accept her situation without any harsh judgment.

The tricky part was the timing for the truth to be revealed. Too early, she reasoned, he would turn away from her. Too late would have the same result, but he would additionally feel that she had been dishonest.

She often found herself thinking, *why can't things just be simple?* But even with the difficulties and dark spots in her life, she was an optimist, and as a Christian she felt truly blessed.

The evening went exceedingly well. At about the exact moment Cain softly kissed her goodnight, Deke passed out on his living room sofa, an empty bottle of Jim Beam's finest on the floor.

The three had achieved their evening goals.

The next morning Jeremy and Ellie awoke in their separate abodes feeling peaceful and happy. They couldn't wait to get to the office to see one another.

Deke on the other hand woke to a pounding headache and his mouth felt like it was full of cotton balls wicking up every bit of moisture he could produce.

His stomach was doing flip-flops as well. He had a major task ahead of him. He needed coffee and lots of it. He made himself eat some dry toast out of fear that he would throw up the coffee if he didn't get something into his belly.

He needed to check his camping gear. He also needed to charge his phone so that he could continue his video log.

A feeling of dread overcame Deke. It stayed with him the entire day. He couldn't shake it. The problem was that he understood why he felt this way, and he didn't like it.

By late afternoon he was entering Rothrock heading towards trailhead three. Twelve minutes later, he was parking at the edge of the clearing where the hikers had camped. He sat in the cab of his truck and stared blankly at the clearing. He remained there immobilized for a full ten minutes.

He finally stirred and climbed out of the cab. He walked the perimeter of the open area. All signs of the attack had been grown over or washed away. As far as nature was concerned, it was just another incident, not even a noteworthy event in the cycle of life and death. Not to be remembered or forgotten. It just was.

He set up a tent that he had no intention of occupying. He created a fire ring and populated it with a few thick dead branches that he would light at dusk. The tent and fire were meant to be a ruse, but he wasn't sure on what level his adversary operated. She may never fall for it. Especially if she were focused on him specifically. And that thought scared him more than he had been in many years.

He attached two trail cams to trees, one on either side of the clearing. Both covered a wide area. They were both high resolution cams and infrared for night viewing. This event, if it occurred, would be captured for posterity.

After all his preparations were complete, he re-entered the cab of the truck and began to record on his phone once again. He recorded for a full twelve minutes. He laid his phone down and opened a sandwich he had packed. He briefly thought, *a condemned man's last meal. A lousy sandwich.* Then his lips parted and he laughed silently to himself.

His next step had him double checking his .45 calibre Heckler and Koch HK45. It was loaded with hollow points and had enough stopping power for almost any North American mammal that he could think of.

He then loaded five 12 gauge shotgun rounds into a magazine and popped it into his Century Arms Catamount Fury II. It was his pride and joy and a woodsman's best friend if trouble were headed his way.

Lastly, Deke set up the final video camera on the back of his pickup. It was a regular HD camera with a low light setting. It was trained upon the tent and fire ring, but its field of vision captured most of the clearing. And with the last light of day waning to almost being imperceptible, he lit the fire in the ring.

To the average person, this was a typical camp setup. He originally thought that he would observe the camp from the cab of his truck, but something told him that was a bad idea. He needed to be the bait in the center of the trap.

Chapter 16

Other Things

Warden Sorenson pulled into an encampment that consisted of two tents, a lean-to, a fire pit and two long tables. This was typical of a poaching setup.

Two deer hung from a thick branch of an old maple tree. It wasn't deer season. Sorenson knew to be extra cautious. The backwoods people could be ruthless.

He considered calling in backup, but that would mean waiting a good hour or more for someone to arrive. Their manpower shortage was aggravating. And Muncy had been their roving man for these three counties and he was gone. God only knows when they'll be able to hire a replacement.

He was on his own and he knew it. There was a job to be done. He needed to be aggressive and let these people know he meant business. He rooted through the glove compartment and brought out four plastic restraints. He also had his pair of handcuffs. He hoped there were no more than five to be dealt with.

He exited his Jeep Cherokee and walked towards the hanging deer. Looking them over he guessed they were taken this very morning.

"Hey, Warden. Good morning."

Startled, he spun around, hand on his pistol.

"Whoa, Chief. No reason to draw your gun," said a pathetically thin, greasy haired man who looked to be in his thirties. He wore bib overalls, a torn sweatshirt and hiking boots.

Sorenson found him disgusting. He looked like a character from Deliverance. His eyes were wild like Jack Nicholson's in The Shining. *He's probably high,* Sorenson thought to himself.

The warden knew this could get ugly quickly if this guy and any others were hopped up on something.

"How do you explain these dead deer?" Sorenson asked.

"Found them. Heard some shooting this morning and went to check it out. These two poor magnificent creatures were lying about forty feet apart. I couldn't let them go to waste, so I dragged them back here," the man lied and smiled.

Sorenson almost threw up. The man's teeth were badly decayed and his saliva looked brown. He figured the man chewed tobacco and right then the man spit a dark brown stream onto the ground.

Sorenson was a good man, but if it were legal he would exterminate vermin like this guy without batting an eye.

"So your skinny ass dragged these deer back by yourself?"

"Naw, Warden. Those two fellers behind you helped me."

Sorenson turned around to find himself on the business end of a shotgun and a deer rifle. The two men were a little fleshier than their tobacco spittin' companion, but just as disgusting.

They wore flannel shirts and blue jeans. Their pants were so caked with grease, blood and grime that calling them blue jeans was just a guess at their original color.

Unlike their skinny partner they were both bearded and looked to be in their forties.

Behind them stood a little girl in a gunny sack dress. She was filthy from head to toe and kept scratching at her shoulder length hair. She held a doll just as grimy as herself.

In those seconds of taking this all in, Sorenson couldn't tell what color her hair was or her age. The poor thing looked as if she had been working in a coal mine.

In those few seconds, Sorenson formulated his plan. He pivoted and ran straight toward the disgusting, skinny clodhopper who had first distracted him. He hoped they wouldn't shoot in the direction of their friend.

He moved so quickly that the tobacco spitter only had time enough to cringe at what was happening. Within seconds Sorensen had him in a headlock and was pointing his Browning 9mm at his friends. He had a human shield, which the good guys weren't supposed to do, but desperate times call for desperate measures against desperate people.

The guy with the shotgun sized things up. He then turned and looked at the little girl and stepped her way. Sorenson knew what he was going to do. Monkey see, monkey do. The bastard was going to use the little girl as his own shield.

Sorenson couldn't let the guy do that or they would have a Mexican standoff that wouldn't end well for him. He fired at the shotgun toter and the man fell to the ground. The slimeball in his headlock squirmed like a greasy pig. The feeling for Sorensen was revolting. He doubled down on his pressure lock and the man became still.

The man with the deer rifle raised his weapon and began sighting in on Sorenson. The warden fired two more times and the man went down hard. He was now feeling better about the odds when a white, hot pain coursed through his back.

He immediately lost the strength in his arms and the greasy man slipped from his grip. The man swung around and said, "give me the knife. I'm gonna finish this bag of shit."

In those few seconds of pain, Sorenson twisted enough to see a filthy, stringy haired woman holding a Buck knife. It was glistening with what he knew was his own blood. This was his swan song.

"Hey, Warden," said the man. "You brought this on yourself." And with that being said, the man swung the Buck knife, which he had taken from the woman, in an arcing motion he slit Sorenson's throat wide open.

The disgusting skinny man checked on his partners. The one with the deer rifle was dead. The shotgun toter was nursing a shoulder wound. He would live.

One more man and woman came running into the camp. They were stunned by what they saw. The woman began to cry. She grabbed the little girl and hurried her away.

The other woman began to patch up the wounded poacher and the other two men argued over who would get the dead man's deer rifle. The tobacco spitter won. And then they buried their fallen comrade.

Afterwards tobacco-spitter handed Sorenson's pistol to the other man as consolation. They then stripped off his uniform and strung him up next to the deer.

The shotgun toter's nursemaid went to the disgusting, skinny man and asked, "Tommy, what the hell you doin' with that fella?"

He responded, "damn it, woman! Meat is meat!"

Cain and Ellie were hard at work in the office. Previously, the warden hated the administrative portion of his duties. He wanted to be out in the field patrolling and interacting with people and nature, but now that all changed. With Ellie present in the office, he didn't want to leave.

It was the middle of the month and his individual warden reports were coming due. The State required a monthly accounting of activity from each warden. In other words, the wardens were required to justify their existence on the payroll.

Cain knew his guys did more than what was required. Justifying themselves was never a problem. The mountain of paperwork was. It took hours and hours to prepare this one report. He hated it. Except now, with Ellie here, it was much more palatable.

All his wardens had faxed in their reports except Sorenson and Vasquez. He picked up the phone and dialed. "Hey, Warden Vasquez. This is your boss. Forget something?"

"Damn, Warden Cain. I've been pulling up fishing traps for the last two days. I forgot all about it. You'll have it in the next half hour. Will that do?"

"Yep. Sounds good and keep up the good work," Cain encouraged.

"I don't know how good the work is, Warden Cain. The backwoods people here call me *The Spanish Devil* or *Warden Diablo*. It's all a matter of perspective," Vasquez quipped.

Cain laughed. He liked Vasquez and had hired him about a year ago. He worked hard and really cared about the job.

They said their goodbyes and Cain dialed again to get Sorenson moving on his report. His cellphone went to voicemail and Cain left a message. This happened often because the wardens were often in areas with no cell service.

He then called Sorenson's home. The warden's wife, Rachel, picked it up on the third ring and sounded breathless.

"Rachel, this is Jeremy Cain. Are you alright?"

"I thought you were Rob or someone calling with bad news."

Cain felt his stomach sink and tighten.

"Rachel, tell me why you were expecting bad news."

"Rob went out yesterday after receiving a call concerning poachers in the abandoned logging section near the western base of Mount Davis. Jeremy, he never came home or called or anything. This happens every now and then, but he warns me first. This time it wasn't planned. Please tell me what to do."

"Rachel, just hold tight. It's probably nothing and he's in a phone dead zone. I'll find him."

He hung up and turned to Ellie who was already waiting for his orders.

"Get Don Denali, Jane Doreemer and Mike Kelso headed this way immediately. And give Salas a call too. I need them here asap. We've got a missing warden."

He then called several Fish and Game volunteer wardens to come in as well. He told them to be in uniform and armed.

Almost two hours later, the group was assembled and ready to go. They had an hour and fifteen minute ride to Forbes State Park, the home of Mount Davis. Mount Davis was the highest spot in Pennsylvania.

The woods in that area were dangerous. Not because of the animals, but because of the hillbillies who populated the area. It was very close to the northwest corner of Maryland and the northeast corner of West Virginia. The people of the region lived by a different code than the average American.

Feuds were still being perpetuated and incest was as rampant as any place in the world. Women fought as often as the men. Children routinely quit school after the sixth grade and young girls became pregnant as young as twelve.

If Sorenson went up on that mountain and upset the balance of their every day lives, then he may be a goner. Cain had often warned him to be careful and ask for help when he needed it.

In fact, Sorenson had used Muncy, Salas and Smith on several occasions. Cain left Ellie in charge of the office. He also asked her to locate Deke and to call Doctor Slocum to get the DNA results from the chunk of the creature they had obtained.

Over an hour later the group was assembled at the old logging site. The first thing they found was Sorenson's Cherokee. It was all locked up and undisturbed.

Cain looked to one of the volunteer wardens. His name was Bear Blackwater. Bear wasn't a nickname. It was his given name as printed on his birth certificate.

"Bear, you're our best tracker. Can you tell us which way he went?"

"Warden Cain, I'll need a few minutes," he answered.

The others got quiet and simply observed Bear go through his ritual.

He searched the ground for obvious signs of boot tracks or disturbed vegetation. He walked through the barren area of stumps left behind by the last logging operation.

At the edge of the forest he knelt down and looked closely at some disturbed vegetation and dead forest detritus. He stood and headed into the forest and disappeared.

Salas looked at Cain and said, "Sir, he knows we're still waiting, right?"

"Yep. He's picked up a track and is verifying it," Cain responded.

Five minutes passed and Bear re-emerged. He waved to the group to follow him and then turned to enter the forest once again.

The group of wardens hurried in his direction. The hunt was on. Bear had definitely gotten the proverbial scent. He was good at this.

Two years ago he found a lost boy. The child was so far into the woods that he never would have found his way home. Bear saved the day.

Bear Blackwater had also found his fair share of escaped criminals. The Pennsylvania State Police used him all the time. Cain would have loved to see Bear become a full-time warden, but he wasn't interested.

Volunteer Warden Blackwater was a taxidermist, one of the best in the area. He was an artist and had done work for several museums, including the Smithsonian.

When Bear heard a warden was missing, he dropped what he was doing. And what he dropped was a life-size diorama for a science museum in Harrisburg. It involved fourteen ducks flying in and landing on the surface of a pond. It was a $70,000 commission. Bear commanded even higher amounts for certain multiple animal attractions.

At the moment he didn't care about any of that. He wanted to find Warden Sorenson. It is the only way that his day would end successfully.

Chapter 17

Wishing For A Different Outcome

Ellie had done everything Cain had asked. Doctor Slocum had news that she found personally gratifying, but it wouldn't make Cain's job any easier. She couldn't wait to share it with him.

On another front, she couldn't raise Deke. He sent her a cryptic email the day before about proving himself. And saying that her and Cain would understand everything because he was making a video diary. This left her confused and a little worried.

Ellie took time to pray for the Warden's effort to find Sorenson. And she prayed that Sorenson be found safe so that he may return to his wife and children.

She had talked to Sorenson several times and had learned that he had what her own father called *a rich man's family*, one boy and one girl. They were, if she remembered correctly, fifteen and thirteen, his son being the oldest.

She thought about her animal studies and nature training and realized that she never knew how dangerous a warden's job was. Wild animals and dangerous people filled the nation's forests. The average person was relatively safe, but the wardens had to confront problems concerning both man and beast.

She thought about Jeremy and prayed that he specifically would be kept safe. She knew he and Sorenson had worked together for quite a while. Jeremy would take it hard if the warden were badly injured or worse.

The phone rang and snapped her away from her dark musings. The caller had questions about camping and hiking and she answered as best she could. That call was quickly followed by another and she became busy with the normal day to day ebb and flow of life in the office. She was grateful for the distractions.

Bear held up his fist. This signaled the other wardens to stop and remain quiet. It also served to remind them that this was a quasi military police action and could become dangerous.

Bear reached for his pistol. The others did the same, except for Denali and Salas who were carrying shotguns. The wardens could not see what Blackwater was seeing. Cain worked his way up beside the tracker.

They were watching two women and a little girl. There were two tents and a lean-to. Under the lean-to was a man lying down with what looked like filthy bandages on his shoulder. Bear tapped Cain on the shoulder and pointed.

Off to the east edge of camp were two men field dressing two deer and a …. Cain wasn't sure he could believe what he was seeing. It looked like Sorenson's dead body was hanging from the tree alongside the deer. He had been gutted, just like the two animals.

The men were were cutting away the fur of the two deer while standing right next to the dead warden as if this was a routine occurrence. The tableau was surreal, like something out of a Wes Craven movie.

Cain moved back to the wardens and had them spread out. The mountain murderers had a radio on which helped to mask their movement. After they were in position, Cain gave the signal and they all moved in.

The camp inhabitants acted as if they never imagined that killing a warden would bring more law enforcement their way. Cain understood it. The wardens were so few and far between that they seemed nonexistent. If you actually saw a warden and killed him, the thinking went there wouldn't be any to take his place.

The women screamed and cried. The little girl stood silent and Cain thought she may be autistic. The men moved toward their weapons, but stopped short, knowing they were outgunned.

The other wardens finally got to see and experience the full impact of seeing Sorenson hanging upside down, gutted and missing a hunk of flesh from his left thigh. Neatly trimmed.

"You son of a bitches!" Salas yelled as he raised the shotgun and poked it squarely in the face of the tobacco spitter. The man presented Salas with an oily grin. Brown, stained rotten teeth made him look less than human. Salas was close to pulling the trigger and sending this pathetic creature straight to hell.

"Warden Salas, stand down! This dog belongs in a cage. That would be the worst punishment for his kind," Cain pleaded.

Salas slowly lowered the shotgun barrel. He knew Cain was right. These hill people wanted to be free and footloose and live outside of any laws. Sticking them in prison would drive them mad, assuming they lasted long enough among the inmate population. Salas figured someone in prison would shiv this piece of shit in the first week.

Restraints were applied to the three men and two women. The little girl was led out by the hand. The hygiene of this band of misfits was deplorable. The smell was sickening.

Cain contacted the State Police to come with a van. This was now a murder investigation on State Forest land. The State Police would now have jurisdiction.

Cain normally would not disturb a crime scene. This time he made an exception. He photographed the deer and Sorenson hanging upside down from the thick tree branch. He documented the posthumous injuries and a deep slice to the warden's throat which he felt was most likely the killing event.

He then allowed his officers to cut Sorenson down. It was too late for Sorenson, but his fellow officers and friends needed to feel that they had re-established honor and dignity for their brother. To some a small gesture, but to the psyche of this group of men it was huge.

They found a blanket in one of the putrid smelling tents. It was filthy, but it re-established modesty for their friend as they covered him up.

Cain sent Denali and Doreemer, along with four volunteer wardens, down to the logging area to await prisoner transfer. He told them to set up a perimeter and not drop their guard. They assumed they had the whole group, but couldn't be sure.

Cain had questioned the group about other members. One of the women said there had been another man, but Sorenson killed him. The tobacco spitter yelled, "shut up, woman!" And the group went silent.

Cain, Kelso and Salas stayed behind. Salas was still fuming and Cain wouldn't let him near the prisoners, although deep down he wanted to.

They awaited the State Police Crime Scene team.

Ellie received a call from Jeremy. He told her they found Sorenson, but he was deceased. He gave no details and asked her to lock up the office when she went home. He would be on-site for many more hours.

She was relieved that he and the others were okay, but hurt deeply for Sorenson's family. She couldn't imagine the pain they would experience.

The afternoon became very slow, so she did some research around Deke's narrative of Penelope's motivation for being active at this time. She really didn't believe the story about the witch, but she had time to kill.

She researched the names of the victims to see how many were descendants of the original area inhabitants, specifically the Canoe Creek area.

One of the hikers was a descendant, Muncy too. All four of the ATV riders were direct descendants and one of the forest crew. She worked at each last name individually and the going was slow.

On her last hit on Google she saw a sight called Canoe Creek's Founders Day. It was an early attempt by a small chamber of commerce to generate pride in their own town. Founders Day was celebrated twice and never caught on as an annual event. What Ellie did find was a list of the original eighteen families that settled the town. There were seventy-one original residents who were deeded the land by French landowners in exchange for the men working the lumber in the area for two years on behalf of the French owners.

The whole affair was rather clandestine since France had ceded most land to the British after it lost the French-Indian War almost fifty years earlier. The whole affair was complicated and Ellie didn't care to try and understand its complexities.

What she was focused upon was that list of original families. She had already traced the victims individually and here was a list confirming her research, but there was a surprise on the list that made her squirm. There was a family named Humboldt.

Deke was a descendant, had something to prove and was missing as far as she was concerned. His email took on a more ominous tone.

Cain had his hands full. She didn't know what to do. She redoubled her efforts to try to raise Deke. She phoned and emailed and waited for a response.

A response would not come.

Chapter 18

The Search For Deke

Cain woke up still exhausted from the previous day's events and the emotional toll it had taken. The last duty that he had last night was to go and tell Sorenson's wife that she was a widow and their children were fatherless.

Rachel Sorenson insisted on details. He begged her not to ask. She demanded to know. He told her the whole story as it was currently understood.

She thanked him and said, "I'm glad he killed one of the bastards. I hope the other guy he shot in the shoulder dies of infection. You can go, Jeremy. There's nothing more you can do for us right now."

She continued, "I feel bad for you. First Muncy's funeral and now you're preparing for my husband's. I hope the State gives you the go ahead to replace them both. You're short-handed as it is. That was Rob's biggest pet peeve."

Cain said goodnight and left. He couldn't believe how strong she was. The tears had run freely down his face as he drove home. His people were dying. He cared deeply, even for Muncy.

Now he lay in bed staring at the ceiling. He wondered if things could get any worse. Thirteen deaths in his woods in a little over a month. Fourteen if you count the hillbilly that Sorenson killed.

He knew that his job was at risk and he didn't care. He wanted to protect people and preserve the natural beauty of what he had been charged to manage. Things had spiraled out of control and he simply didn't have the resources he needed.

His wardens should be riding in pairs for their safety and to do the job more efficiently. The State had his hands tied, and for a moment he allowed himself to be angry over how long he would have to wait for replacements for Muncy and Sorenson.

Cain then felt a moment of shame for thinking only of himself. That wasn't who he was. He got himself out of bed and prepared to go into the office. Maybe seeing Ellie would brighten his mood. He hoped that seeing him didn't bring her mood down.

Twenty-five minutes later he walked into the office. Ellie ran to him and gave him a hug.

"Jeremy, I'm so sorry. Truly I am."

"We need to stop all the killing in these woods. People are going to start feeling unsafe in our State Forests. Can't have that," he said with conviction.

She handed him a newspaper. The front page headline read:

Death Toll In PA Woodlands Becomes An Epidemic
The sub-headline read:
Law Enforcement Out-Manned, Out-Gunned And Out Of Ideas

"Where in the hell did they get this piece of crap?" Cain yelled. He read further. The reporter had talked to an unnamed State Forestry spokesperson.

The unnamed source provided the facts about how budgetary constraints had made it nigh impossible to police and protect the citizens of Pennsylvania in her forested areas. He was stunned how bold the source was and how accurate they were as well. No wonder they remained anonymous.

"I did what you wanted while you were gone yesterday," Ellie said trying to get his mind off the article. She wished she had never shown it to him in the first place.

"How's that? What I wanted?"

"Yes. I talked to Doctor Slocum. The DNA confirms that the animal is a great ape species. Unclassified as far as he can tell. So congratulations, were dealing with a Bigfoot. He's going to call it *Slocum Erectus*."

"I don't care what he calls it. I just want to find it and kill it."

"Oh no! You can't. It's a new species. You can't just kill it. It probably already meets the requirements for being endangered. Catch it, but don't kill it," she pleaded.

He looked at her angrily. "Are you kidding me? All these people dead because of it and your first reaction is to protect it? Holy shit, Ellie! Decide which species you prefer. I prefer human with a capital H. No ifs, ands or buts!"

"Well, did your humans make you proud yesterday?" she shot back at him. She wished she could have taken the words back as soon as they left her mouth. She saw the look of hurt play across his face.

He looked at her and said, "take the rest of the day off. I need to handle a volatile situation and I need people around me who are on my side."

"Jeremy, I'm sorry. Please forgive me. I know you're hurting and I am on your side. No one is more on your side than me."

"Then why haven't you told me about your son? Or that your husband is in prison? It doesn't feel like you're on my side at all," he said with a sigh.

"Ex-husband. Ex. And I didn't feel we were yet at the point where that was critical. I wanted you to know me before you swept me aside. Yes, I have a beautiful four year old boy. He lives with his grandparents while I concentrate on making something of myself so I can take care of him without help."

"I guess you didn't owe me the truth. I'm just a warden that you're interning with. Thanks for the good work you have been doing." He then headed for the door.

"Jeremy, STOP! Deke's missing."

He turned with a wild look on his face. "What do you mean he's missing? That should have been the first damn thing out of your mouth."

"I didn't want to overreact. He doesn't answer my calls, texts or emails. He could be out too far for a signal. You once said he disappears for days at a time, right?" she explained.

"You're right. I am a bit on edge. He does go missing out in the woods from time to time, but it is a little more dangerous right now. Oh hell, who am I kidding? It's a lot more dangerous. Your pet Bigfoot may be out there with him."

"Kill it! I don't care! I care about you, Deke and all the wardens. I really am sorry for what I said. I study animals to keep them alive using conservation methods. But this thing is different. It kills people. I get it."

There was an uncomfortable moment of silence between them. Neither was sure how to come back from the current awkward situation.

"I'd like to meet your little boy," he blurted out.

"Does that mean you don't hate me?" she asked.

"Just the opposite, Ellie. Just the opposite."

She lunged forward and wrapped her arms around his neck. She rested her forehead against his lips and quietly whispered, "me too, Jeremy."

He gently pushed her away and declared, "we need to put this on hold until we find Deke. He is actually my best friend. And I won't rest until we find him."

Ellie told Jeremy about the strange email. Cain hadn't checked his own email for at least two days.

He sat in front of his computer and started it up so that he could check his .gov account. That was the one Deke used to contact him.

As they waited for his computer to work through updates, Ellie provided one more piece of information.

"Jeremy, the Humboldts are also part of the Canoe Creek founding families. Deke is a descendent."

"Ellie, why do I feel nauseated. I think that man has me believing in witches."

"Me too. I hate to admit it, but Bigfoot to witches isn't that much of a leap on the belief scale."

He began typing. Minutes later he looked at her and said, "call Salas and Smith. Have them meet us at Rothrock."

Once again the wardens had to drive a long distance to back each other up. It pissed Cain off to high heaven. He had this luxury, right now, of being within an hour of three different wardens. That fact happened to be coincidental to where the wardens found homes. They each had territory to cover where they were alone and out of reach.

The farther north and west his counties extended, his men and women were working solo. It was too dangerous. After this current situation was resolved, he promised himself he would work tirelessly to have the budget increased so that his counties could have more floaters for backup.

He and Ellie reached Rothrock first. Specifically they were headed to trailhead 3. They waited for their backup at the park entrance off of Route 22.

Forty-five minutes passed before Salas showed up. Another fifteen passed and Smith pulled into the entrance area.

Their three car convoy headed towards the trailhead at a rapid rate. Cain was beginning to feel the first tugs of panic setting in. He already knew this wasn't going to go well.

They saw Deke's truck pulled onto the berm of the trail road. In the clearing, they saw a tent laying about in shredded pieces. The ground was covered in patches of crimson. Salas was the first to notice Deke lying on his side about thirty feet away from the treeline.

Cain ran full bore to the spot Salas had pointed to. He slipped in some bloody fragments, presumably belonging to Deke. The body looked at first to be intact. Cain knelt down and rolled him over.

Deke's face was gone. His right arm was partially chewed off. Claw marks were visible where he had been disemboweled. This was a different kind of attack.

Cain stared down at what was left of his friend. The pressure had reached beyond what any man could tolerate. He thought, *Muncy, Sorenson and now Deke.*

Cain sat down in the grass holding Deke and cried. Ellie came over to him, kneeled and began to rub his back. Salas and Smith understood their boss's reaction completely.

They stayed back, not because they were embarrassed by this emotional display, but because they needed to provide protection against an unknown assailant. They knew they needed to maintain a perimeter.

It took Cain a full fifteen minutes to work through his emotional response. Once he was composed, he stood and walked over to his wardens. "Salas, call this in to the medical examiner's office. Then we'll walk the scene. Smith, check Deke's truck for clues. Find something that would make sense of this."

Ellie looked at the torn and bloodied husk that used to be Deacon Humboldt. She felt so empty. She had liked him very much and she realized she would never see him again. It seemed surreal to her.

She didn't even react to how revolting his corpse looked because she was too overcome with the grief. And her concern was focused on Jeremy. This was his best friend.

His temporary breakdown made her love him even more. He somehow had found the inner strength to take charge again. He was a remarkable man.

"Warden Cain!" yelled Smith. "I found something in the truck!"

Cain hurried over to Deke's truck. Smith handed him an envelope. On the outside, handwritten in block letters, it read, *To Ranger Cain*.

Cain smiled at first and then tears came. Even in death Deke was being his usual asshole self.

Cain whispered, "Stop calling me Ranger."

"You okay, sir?" Smith asked.

Cain didn't answer immediately. He took a few deep breaths and said, "I'm fine. Let's see what is in the envelope."

He opened it up. It was a printed letter from Deke. This is what it said:

> *Dear Warden Cain (see I can remember),*
> *If you are reading this I am dead or at least severely*
> *injured. You will find two HD infra-red trail cams mounted*
> *on the trees with the spray painted orange exes. A standard*
> *HD video camera is mounted in the bed of my truck.*
> *All are motion activated. Each has a 128gb smart card to*
> *record the proceedings. I sincerely hope these devices will*
> *record my attackers and help you deal with this before*
> *anyone else is hurt or killed.*
> *Good luck.*
>
> *Cain, your friendship has meant the world to me. See my*
> *lawyer, Marvin Greenbaum in Altoona. He has my will and*
> *you're getting everything.*
> *Consider it my wedding gift to you and Ellie. Yes Cain,*

*marry the girl. Anyone can see you two are an
awesome fit.*

Don't screw it up, dammit.

*And if you don't marry her (fool) you can keep my
shit*

anyway. See you in the funny papers.

*Your friend,
Deke*

Ellie wandered over just as Cain began reading the letter. She was reading it over his shoulder.

Cain turned to her with eyes still brimming with tears. "I don't know what's wrong with me. I can't seem to get myself under control. I'm sorry."

"Don't be. You lost someone you cared about deeply. If you didn't cry, I'd worry about you," she said softly.

"What do you think we ought to do about the wedding gifts?" he smiled.

"Why don't you meet my son first. If he doesn't like you then you're history," she smiled back and then paused as if thinking. "Actually, I think Deke was pretty perceptive."

Salas had joined them. "Sorry about your friend. Loss is all we seem to be getting thrown at us lately."

"Gentleman, we need to retrieve two trail cams on the trees with the orange exes. I'll grab the one here in the bed of the truck." He took a step and looked down. "What's this?"

"Oh sorry, boss," said Salas. "That, I assume, is Deke's shotgun. It's a beaut. Five-round magazine completely emptied and I found these." He reached into his pocket and produced two expended shotgun shells.

Ellie spoke up. "He's wearing a holster, but there was no gun in it."

"Okay, get the cameras. Then we'll walk the entire area."

Forty minutes passed before the ME's vehicle pulled into the trailhead. During that time they found Deke's pistol. It appeared to have been fired, but several bullets remained in the magazine and one in the chamber.

Two more of the five shotgun shells were also found. A massive amount of blood had been dispersed. Almost too much for one two hundred and fifty pound man.

There was a patch of vegetation that was flattened and then tore up quite a bit and scraped in spots. They couldn't wait to examine the cameras.

Two bear tracks were also found, but they could have been made anytime over the last two or three days. It was obvious that Deke made a stand, but against what they weren't sure.

The ME himself was on this trip. His name was Doctor Milton Rosen. He made his way over to Cain, "Warden, you guys are having a patch of bad luck lately. Do you have any clues as to what is doing this?"

Cain had dealt with Rosen before. He was a self important, arrogant little prick. It was obvious that he came out on this particular run to pick up the body so that he'd have some interesting fodder for his many cocktail parties.

Cain glared at him. "Doctor, do you believe in monsters?"

"No, of course not," he answered.

"You better start," declared Cain and then he walked away leaving the ME in stunned silence.

Chapter 19

The Video

Cain told Smith and Salas they could leave if they wanted to. They had thoroughly examined the area and taped it off. The State Police had signed off on it as another animal attack, so it was Cain's investigation.

Salas asked, "are you going back to the office to look at the pictures and video?"

"Yes, why?" answered Cain.

"Because wild horses couldn't drag me away from looking at those with you," he shot back. Smith was in agreement and shook his head enthusiastically for all to see.

They hopped into their vehicles and headed to the Canoe Creek office. All were chomping at the bit to see what had really happened. Deep down, they all knew they were about to see what was murdering people in their woods. They yearned for this nightmare to stop.

They were about to find out what nightmares are really made of.

Once at the office, Cain and Ellie worked on Cain's laptop and inserted the smartcard from the video recorder. Smith and Salas used Ellie's desktop computer to begin looking at the trail cam snapshots.

The video clicked to life. It showed Deke holding his shotgun and narrating what was happening.

"I just heard a horrible screeching yell. It wasn't too far away." The video continues for a few minutes then the shrieking occurs again. "It's closer now."

Smith and Salas just had stills of Deke standing and holding his shotgun so far.

"Just saw something white moving between the trees. Not sure what it is." A few moments went by.

Salas spoke up, "We got what looks like a woman running at the edge of the clearing. She's got long hair and wearing a long white or light colored dress of some sort. It appears Deke is looking in her direction."

The video continues. "Who are you?" Deke shouts.

The shriek that presumably emanates from the woman is so loud that the sound equipment of the camera becomes tinny and indistinct. Even so, the sound makes Ellie and Jeremy cringe and begin to feel unnerved.

"What on God's green earth is that? It's huge and it's coming…" Deke can be seen raising his shotgun and firing several times. The attacker enters the video just as it is falling down. The shotgun hit its mark. The thing appears to be huge and fur covered.

Salas screams, "you guys gotta see this!"

Cain stops the video and he and Ellie join Salas and Smith.

Smith says, "look at that thing in relationship to the branch heights. It has to be eight or nine feet tall. Remember that small pine tree that stands alone by the big rock pile? It's right next to it. Unbelievable."

"It's on two legs. That'll make Doc Slocum happy," Cain said truly in awe of what they were witnessing. "In our video, Deke shot it. Jump ahead to see if that was captured."

It was. The creature appears to break into a run. The shots capturing it is only a few frames long which proves it was incredibly fast. It appeared to favor one side over another. Maybe it was wounded, each of them thought separately.

The trail cam caught a flair from Deke's raised shotgun three times. That coincided with the video. The creature goes down in only two frames and then it is still.

Deke appears to walk around it. Nudges it with his shotgun. No movement of the beast is recorded.

Smith whistled and said, "damn. Deke killed freaking Chewbacca! Way to go, dude."

"If Deke killed the thing, then what killed Deke?" Cain got up and walked back to the video and started it again.

"Guys, this is huge. It's dead, but Penelope is still around here somewhere." As Deke says this for the camera, Cain sees her standing ten feet behind Deke. She screams maxing out the audio again.

Ellie, Salas and Smith hear the narrative and gather around Cain's laptop. The screech has brought Deke to his knees holding his ears. He must have dropped the shotgun. Then he picks it up and stands a little shakily. He spins and is face to face with Penelope, only five feet between them.

"I didn't kill you, bitch. I had nothing to do with it. Go away. Go back to whatever hell you've been stuck in."

A roar is heard off camera. They can see Deke pivot. He raises the shotgun again and fires a shot.

"Damn cat. It's a mountain lion!" he says in a loud voice. "A big son of a bitch."

A low growl can be heard. Another roar, but this isn't a cat.

Deke looks toward the sound. "Holy shit! A bear! Guys, I've got a bear and a mountain lion who want to play!"

He fires the shotgun from his hip towards the bear. He drops that gun and pulls his Koch HK45. Cain notices Penelope hasn't moved. Deke has moved away from her slightly. Maybe ten feet separates them, and she is still to his rear.

Deke is sizing up his targets. Penelope stiffens and holds her arms down at her sides and screams. Deke fires one shot in the mountain lion's direction and drops to his knees again, holding his ears.

It is then over in seconds. The mountain lion enters the camera frame stage left at a high rate of speed and is on him in seconds. The bear can now be seen lumbering in at a fast pace and joins the fray. Cain hits pause.

"It's okay, sir. We can look at the rest. There's no need for you to go through this all again. You and Ellie can take a break."

Ellie hugged Jeremy tight around his shoulders. "Warden Smith is right. Let them get past this part."

Jeremy stood up and said, "I don't want to see any more of his death, unless something or someone else enters the picture. But what I do want to know is how that beast could appear dead, but not be there when we arrived? Tell me when you see the answer to that." He then walked out and stood on the porch. Ellie was right behind him.

"Sorry, Ellie. I guess I'm not acting very manly today. I feel like I'm about to explode. We just witnessed proof positive that another kind of creature lives in those woods and I want them all dead. I want to find and kill that bear and that mountain lion, and if I knew how to kill a dead witch, I'd go after her too."

"I understand. I really do. If that had been you in the video, I would feel exactly the same way," she said.

"And on a selfish note, it sure sucks falling in love in the midst of all this tragedy. I've waited a long time to experience this again and now it seems tainted."

"Were you ever married before?"

"Yes. Two years."

She asked, "divorce?"

"Nope. Drunk driver."

"Oh, Jeremy. I'm so sorry."

"And before you ask, no kids. Just a gaggle of nieces and nephews whom I spoil at every chance."

"My son is going to like you. I'm sure of it."

"And if he doesn't?"

"What does he know? He's just a kid."

They both laughed. It felt strange under the circumstances, but it also felt good. Jeremy needed a light moment.

The door flew open.

"Holy shit, guys! You have to see this! You won't believe it!" Salas said breathlessly.

They hurried back in to crowd around Smith and the laptop.

"You guys ready? Deke has been deceased for about twenty minutes when this happens."

They saw Penelope, at least that was who they agreed she was, standing at the edge of the clearing. She stiffens up once again with her hands at her side and shrieks.

The bear and the big cat are hunched over Deke feasting and they stop. They slowly circle Bigfoot and then appear to close in to dine on that creature as well. But they didn't.

"Watch this," Salas said.

Each creature grabs ahold of a separate huge arm and begin to pull the Bigfoot towards the woods. The video continues for another seventeen minutes as they disappear into the forest.

"You must be shitting me," Cain said softly. "I feel like I should just sit in a corner and drool into a cup. I don't know a thing about nature. This proves it."

"Jeremy, there better be room in that corner. This is my point of emphasis and no one even hinted that this could occur," Ellie added.

Salas asked the question they were all afraid to ask. "Now what, sir?"

"In the morning I'll call Slocum and meet with him and go over this video evidence. Then I'll ask him to put a team together, including a tracker, and go into those woods and find Chewbacca's corpse. After that I'll find someone who has knowledge of the paranormal. I'll probably end the day sitting alone in my apartment getting drunk as a skunk because this isn't anywhere close to being the real life I was taught to handle."

"What about tonight?" Ellie asked.

"How about a pizza? That's a really normal thing to do. Pizza and a pitcher of beer. Salas and Smith, I would normally invite you to come along, but apparently her and I are falling in love and I want alone time. Kapisch?"

"You got it, sir. We'll just scurry back to our own holes and not bother you until you need us," Smith laughed.

With that the day ended and the evening began.

The pizza was from a mom and pop pizza joint called The Leaning Tower of Pizza. It was delicious. The conversation stayed light at first and then Jeremy told Ellie that maybe they should have an early night. He couldn't get

Deke out of his mind and he was truly at a loss about how to proceed with the investigation in light of the incredible circumstances that surrounded it.

She agreed. They had driven separately. He walked her to her car and kissed her goodnight. They looked longingly into each others' eyes. Ellie was the first to speak.

"Can we go slow regarding the physical part of our relationship? My ex-husband ruined that aspect for me for a long time. I want to be totally ready when we broach that part of our being together. And Jeremy, it will happen. Often I hope, but I have to be ready."

"Thank you. Right now I agree that part can wait. I'm too mentally distracted to be my best. Right now I just need a loving friend."

"Well, it was a pleasure not sleeping with you," she said.

"Same to you, madam."

Five minutes later they headed towards their own homes.

Chapter 20

Slocum Becomes Helpful

Cain made an appointment to see Doctor Slocum at his office on campus. Once their meeting began, Slocun could do nothing but sit in stunned, almost gleeful silence, as he viewed the video.

When it was finished, he said, "Warden Cain, I am truly sorry about the loss of your friend. This man, Deacon Humboldt, has done the scientific community the greatest service possible. This is irrefutable proof and his own death testifies to its validity.

"But if you'll forgive me, who in God's name is the screaming woman? And how did those animals work in concert to conceal the giant beast?"

"Well, Doctor. We believe the woman is a two hundred year old dead witch seeking revenge against the living. She is controlling the animals in this video," Cain explained.

Slocum spoke. "Do you really expect me to believe that? I mean, the video would surely support part of your claim, but that's a stretch, even for a Bigfoot believer like myself."

"Doc, I don't need you to believe in the witch right now. I just need for you to put together a search party and find that thing's corpse. Can you do that?"

"Consider it done, Warden Cain. I have friends in Tyrone who have tracking dogs. We'll find this beast if it is still out there," the doctor promised.

"Where else would it be, Doctor Slocum?"

"Warden, a Bigfoot corpse has never ever been found before. So your guess is as good as mine. But I'll get right on it."

"One other thing I must insist on Doctor. When you're ready, call this man. He's one of my best men. He needs to be with you every step of the way," Cain insisted as he handed a card to Slocum.

"Warden Richard Salas. Okay, Warden Cain. It would probably be a good thing to have an armed escort in light of recent events. I'll call him as soon as I have everyone scheduled."

Cain thanked the doctor and left. He had one more stop on campus. He had an appointment with a professor in the Anthropology department.

He made his way across the sprawling campus to the Founders Hall building. There he was shown into the office of Professor Rita Alcorn. He was told she would be along in a few minutes. She was finishing up a meeting with a group of grad students.

He looked at her small office with a mixture of disgust and awe. A pre-Columbian fertility statue was poised on the corner of her desk. It stood about twelve inches tall with an erect five inch penis sticking straight out the front.

This woman was either trolling for sexual partners or she was clueless as to how this may be perceived. Cain couldn't wait to find out.

The shelves in her office were filled with the requisite academic tomes. Charts of hominid family trees were all over the walls. It was quite obvious the woman believed we were descended from monkeys. Yet, a contradictory image was hanging on the wall. A ten inch

Catholic crucifix was attached to the wall behind and to the left of her desk.

Cain made himself chuckle thinking that the woman he was about to meet was a horny Catholic evolutionist.

"Something amusing, Warden Cain?" said a voice from behind him.

He stood and turned to see a little five foot nothing, no nonsense pit bull of a woman staring at him. He was so startled by her appearance that he almost jumped.

"No, Ma'am. Nothing is funny at all."

"You have twenty minutes. No more. I'm between classes."

"Your name was given to me by a man named Deacon Humboldt about a month ago."

"Oh, Old Deke. How's he doing?"

"Dead," he paused for dramatic effect, "which is why I'm here."

She, as he expected, looked stunned.

"What happened, Warden Cain? Nothing horrible I hope."

"Actually, Professor, it's about as horrible as you can imagine. He was torn apart by both a bear and a mountain lion."

"Oh my. Two separate attacks, obviously."

"No, Ma'am. One coordinated attack."

"You are telling me a bear and a mountain lion colluded to attack a human being? That's ridiculous."

"I have it on film."

"Oh my. This becomes more preposterous by the second. So somehow someone was filming this event? Why didn't they stop it? How could they film it and not do something?"

"Because Deke set up the equipment around his encampment before they attacked."

"Are you saying he knew he was going to be attacked?"

"Yes, Ma'am. In a way he did. He just wasn't sure by what."

"Warden, I really must be going soon, so get to your point if you have one."

The person behind Deke's death, and several others, is a witch that has been dead for two hundred years."

"Penelope Sutter? The unfortunate bride from Canoe Creek? Deke was stuck on that story recently," she said, explaining how she knew.

"Yes, Ma'am," Cain said politely.

"Young man, if you *yes, Ma'am* me one more time, I'm going to shove that statue's penis up your nose. Call me professor, or since you knew Deke, you can call me Rita."

Cain was caught off guard by her threat and began to laugh.

"I see we're back to finding something amusing," she said with a slight smirk on her face.

"Please, call me Jeremy. Deke was my best friend. Obviously he talked to you about Penelope. Why?"

"I run the campus chapter of Parapsychology America. It's open to anyone and Deke became a member a few years ago. And as I stated, recently he became obsessed with Penelope's story."

"I have a video I need you to look at. When is your next class over?"

"Jeremy, I don't have another class today. I lied so I could get you to leave when I had had enough. Please forgive me. People, mostly students, are at me all the time. My free time is a precious commodity. Now lets look at your video."

Cain warned her it was Deke's death they would be watching and it was gruesome. He also prepared her to suspend disbelief on two fronts, but he left it vague as to what exactly he meant. He plugged in a thumbdrive and started the video on her computer.

She watched in total silence. Jeremy couldn't discern her reaction to the video by any facial expressions or ticks. He thought to himself, *I wouldn't want to play poker with this woman. She gives nothing away.*

Twenty-two minutes later the video was complete. The professor looked at him and let out a long stream of air through pursed lips.

"Well?" he prodded.

"Jeremy, you're in deep shit, if you pardon my French. A ghost, Bigfoot and two wild animals. All natural enemies, working together to do what appears to be the ghost's bidding. Amazing. Did you find the big thing's body?"

"There is a team being formed to do just that. Do you know Doctor Slocum?"

"I've seen him. A very quiet man from what I have noticed," she answered.

"That's because he got crucified out on the West Coast by academia because of his interest in Bigfoot. He is trying to stay off the radar. That may change soon. Anyway, he's putting a team together to accompany one of my wardens on a search for the beast's corpse."

"So what exactly do you want from me?" she queried.

"I want you to go after Penelope."

She stared at him. Once again, he could discern nothing from her look.

"Why should I?"

"Rita, I just brought you the most conclusive proof of both Bigfoot and a vengeful ghost. If you are truly interested in the study of the paranormal, how could you not want to join us?"

"She looks a little dangerous. In fact, if she is responsible for all the deaths I've been reading about in the last month or so, she's definitely dangerous."

"Yes, but Penelope no longer has her big monkey. That thing was her main weapon. At least that's what I believe."

"And if you're wrong, Jeremy? She seemed to have fair control of a bear and a mountain lion. As far as you know she could control a colony of beavers and have them slap you to death with their tails."

Jeremy burst into laughter. The image of killer beavers was what he needed to relieve his tension. "Well, if she uses beavers, just don't enlist anyone with wooden legs."

Now it was Rita's turn to laugh.

"Okay, Jeremy. I'm on-board. Give me a couple of days to read up on witch lore. That will give us a starting point for dealing with Penelope. That is, if she is actually a witch. What if she is really just a pissed off two hundred year old bride?"

"Deke recited a saying from the part of the video that I didn't show you. I wrote it down. It's right here in my wallet." He pulled his wallet from his back pants pocket, removed a folded piece of paper and read it aloud,

"Good witch ere a dead witch
On this count tis true
Unless she return
On century two
Old lines of blood
No revenge will delay
The spawn of her killers
All debt must repay"

"That's rather illuminating since this is the two hundredth anniversary of her death," Cain provided.

"Deke knew more about the witch aspects of paranormal research than I or most others did. He was fascinated with witches, warlocks, shaman, medicine men and voodoo priests.

"And like I said, Jeremy, I need to brush up on a few things. Plus, I have several colleagues for which this falls right into their area of interest. I should be ready to suit up, so to speak, in about two days. I'll call you when I'm ready," she concluded.

They shook hands. Cain gave her his card and they said their goodbyes. Everything was moving forward.

Chapter 21

A Big Body

Jack and Amy had two bloodhounds, Molly and Shep. They had trained the dogs from ten weeks to their current age of four years. From the same litter, Molly and Shep showed an amazing ability to work together as a team.

The brother and sister never muffed an assignment. Missing children, escaped fugitives or plastic Easter eggs with treats hidden inside, the pair always came through.

Jack and Amy were husband and wife. They worked together well also. It was living together that posed their greatest challenge. Their interest in dogs was what drew them close. And after a hasty courtship, the dog handlers married. They found that they didn't have much else in common beyond their love for their canine companions.

Jack was an avid sports fan and outdoorsman. Amy hated sports and preferred the creature comforts of home. Jack wanted children. Amy wanted more dogs and the freedom that motherhood would surely squash. Working the dogs was truly their only common ground. For now it was enough, but they both knew their marriage wasn't going to last much longer.

After a few rough weeks together, the call from Doctor Slocum was a godsend. The dogs were needed to track an animal that was believed to be dying or dead. Slocum had been rather vague as to the species, which they both found a bit strange.

Their concern was for the safety of their animals. They would have to press him a little once they got on-site. The meeting place was Rothrock State Forest near trailhead three.

Jack and Amy both kept up with the local news and both wondered if they would be tracking the animal or animals responsible for the recent deaths. Both had permits to carry weapons and they decided this was a time when it would be prudent to do so.

Armed with the GPS coordinates that Doctor Slocum provided, they were on their way.

Doctor Slocum was already standing at the trailhead with Warden Salas and three grad students looking to score points with a faculty member. None of the three knew what the nature of their quest was. Slocum wanted it that way.

Doctor Slocum wanted full and complete credit for what he hoped would be the inevitable discovery. Grad students are easily hushed and manipulated. Warden Salas and the dog team would be no problem. In fact, the only thing that had him concerned was the shotgun that Salas carried. It was a cannon.

The fact was that Salas was carrying Deke's Century Arms Catamount Fury II. Cain made sure that Salas had it for this venture, just in case. Salas knew this was only a search and recovery mission during full daylight, but he had to admit that he felt more secure carrying it.

The dog team pulled into a spot behind the warden's vehicle. The dog handlers obviously had a sense of humor. The sign on the side of their van had three giant letters that stood out reading from top to bottom, CAT.

Beside each letter was the rest of each word, Canine Assistance Team. Salas thought it was pretty clever.

The CAT team unpacked their equipment, including two dogs that Salas recognized from when he was a very small child. His parents loved the old show The Beverly Hillbillies. Uncle Jed's dogs were out and sniffing around.

So far the dog team was providing Salas with quite a bit of amusement. He hoped they were capable of doing the job that they came to do. He would like to know for sure that the giant beast was dead. It was very personal for all the wardens.

Jack walked over to Salas, "Ranger, the name is Jack. That's my wife Amy. Could you please fill us in as to the nature of the animal we're tracking."

Warning bells went off in Salas' head. *They didn't know what they came to look for,* Salas thought. *What the hell?*

He thought of Deke and Cain before he spoke. "For starters, don't call me Ranger. I am Warden Salas and I'm pleased to meet you. To answer your question, you are here to track a Sasquatch."

Jack's mouth opened, but no words issued forth. Amy walked up and said, "Honey, did they tell you what we're looking for?" Amy turned to Salas. "I'm Amy, by the way." She extended her hand in greeting. Salas politely shook it.

"Warden Salas, would you tell her what you told me?" Jack said with a smirk.

"Sure," Salas responded. "We're searching for Bigfoot." Salas informed her in his most deadpan fashion.

She smiled at Jack. He looked down and shook his head.

"You're serious? Or is this a college prank? Because if it is, we are still charging you for our time and travel," Amy informed Salas indignantly.

Slocum walked over and said, "Jack, Amy, you both look upset. What's wrong?"

"Bigfoot, Doctor Slocum? Are you shitting me?"

"I wish I could have explained before someone told you. If you have been following the news…" he began and then recounted everything, including Deke's death. By the time Slocum was done filling their heads with the publicity and fame they would receive as part of the team, they were almost ready to pay to be part of the hunt.

Salas watched the whole thing. He had to admit, Slocum told a good story. Everyone was now primed and ready to go.

Slocum pulled out a plastic bag containing some hair and Amy held it in front of the dogs. The dogs sniffed and snuffled over the bag and then immediately headed towards the exact spot where the bear and lion had dragged the beast. They were on the scent. The hunt had begun.

Jeremy occupied himself with a mountain of paperwork. He had just come from Draper's Funeral Home. Deke had no family left. No kids, no siblings and parents deceased.

Marvin Greenbaum, attorney-at-law, had informed Jeremy that Deke's wishes were that he was to be cremated. No service. He requested his ashes be scattered in the Little Juniata River.

Jeremy only needed to arrange the cremation and pickup of the ashes. No service and no urn made Cain's input perfunctory.

His friend's absence continued to feel unreal.

The previous day found Cain and Ellie attending Sorenson's funeral. His wife and children were devastated. He was a good man. Cain would miss him.

A funeral one day and a funeral home the next. His life was tending towards tragedy at the moment. He knew Salas was out with Slocum's group. He hoped to hear from Rita today. He felt confident that he asked the right person to help. He reasoned if Deke trusted her why shouldn't he.

Ellie wasn't in the office today. She had a dentist appointment along with her son. After that it was going to be a mom and son day. She threatened to stop by to introduce Cain. He was actually nervous. He knew that if the child took a disliking to him he was doomed.

The day wore on. He was waiting for Salas or Slocum to call, waiting for Rita to call and waiting for Ellie to stop by. He wondered at what point did his life become about everyone else.

At about 2:30 pm the phone rang.

"Over here, Professor!" shouted Jack. "We've got something!"

Everyone came running from all directions. The dogs were sniffing a large, crudely formed mound of loose dirt.

Salas' first thought was, *there's no freaking way those animals buried the thing. That's too creepy.*

Slocum asked the grad students to begin removing the dirt. None of them had a shovel. They looked around and found some branches to begin the dirt removal.

Within five minutes a female grad student named Tina screamed and stepped back. Everyone else stepped forward.

There sticking out from the dirt was a hand. It wasn't a paw. It had four elongated digits and what appeared to be a long thumb. Each digit was tipped by a black looking nail or claw. Bigfoot had been discovered.

The grad students bent their backs to their work with more energy and excitement. The entire creature was slowly emerging.

Salas was thinking the thing looked bigger in person than it did on the video. It looked to be every bit of eight feet. He wondered how many more of these things were roaming the woods.

And then he surprised himself by thinking, *if Penelope found one, she could find another.* He paused, shook his head and said, "oh my God! I believe this shit!"

Slocum sidled up next to him. "Isn't this wonderful, Warden Salas?"

"Sure. Great. Just freaking great," he replied.

Ellie walked into the office with her son. Cain was relieved to see her. He looked at the little boy. A cuter little fella he had never seen.

He looked a little small for his age. He had big blue eyes and blonde hair in a bowl-style haircut.

"Joshua, this is Warden Cain. He's in charge of all the State Forests in this part of the state. You know, where all the animals live and play," Ellie explained.

Joshua looked up and smiled and then he saw Jeremy's gun and stepped back behind his mom's leg. Jeremy saw his reaction plain as day.

He removed his holster and placed it in a drawer.

"There, buddy, the gun's gone," Jeremy got down on his haunches and extended his hand for a handshake.

Joshua slowly moved forward and grabbed his hand.

"Wow, what a grip, kiddo. You're strong," Jeremy complimented.

Joshua smiled, revealing deep dimples. Jeremy felt himself falling for the kid faster than he did for his mother. *What a cutie,* he thought.

"Ahem, Mom is here too. Remember me?"

"Oh, it's you. When did you walk in?"

"Very funny," she said as she stepped forward and kissed him.

Cain then gave Jeremy a little tour. Ellie was delighted by their interaction. When they finished, Jeremy came up with a box of crayons and a coloring book called *Forest Friends.*

"What do you say, young man?" Ellie prompted him.

"Thank you, sir." He then got down to the business of adding color to the pages.

"Anything going on?" Ellie asked, turning her attention to Jeremy.

"Just got a call from Salas. Bigfoot has been recovered. He says the thing is darn near the size of his car."

"What does he drive?"

"He drives a Honda Fit. He had to call a friend of his who owns a John Deere tractor with a bucket. Seven people couldn't drag it, but a bear and mountain lion did.

Of course, he said the two women wouldn't touch it. So actually, five people couldn't move the thing."

"Sounds scary," she offered.

"That's nothing. Things are going to go crazy around here. Get ready for a media circus. And I am expecting Bigfoot hunters to fill our forests."

"Will that be a problem?"

"Yes and no. The increased number of people out there may keep Penelope under wraps. Of course, the problem will be a bunch of armed nuts filling the woods. Now that's scary."

"How does it keep Penelope under wraps?"

"I don't know. Wishful thinking on my part. I am hoping she'll be confused by all the activity."

"Can't you ask Slocum to keep it quiet for a while?"

"I did. He said *no way*. This is his vindication and gives him a chance to thumb his nose at his West Coast critics. To be honest, I can't blame him."

"Oh, Jeremy, your job is going to get so much harder."

"Yeah, I'll probably need some serious stress relief," he said as he winked at her.

"Easy tiger. We're taking that part slow, remember?"

Jeremy smiled his most charming smile and whined, "but I'm really stressed."

Ellie rolled her eyes and said, "oh, shut up! You men are all alike."

They both smiled and laughed at their playfulness.

Joshua looked up at them and asked, "what's so funny, Mommy?"

"Warden Cain is funny, dear. He is hilarious."

Joshua looked at them both and began laughing, which prompted Jeremy and Ellie to join him. It was a good first meeting with the boy. They were all happy.

It wouldn't last.

Chapter 22

Dem Old Bones

"I'm glad you have a plan, Rita. Do you want to let me in on it?"

"Sure, Jeremy, maybe you can help. My people insist that we need to find Penelope's bones. If we can find her earthly remains, we may be able to have some control over her."

"And how, pray tell, do you find two hundred year old bones in the forest?"

"With a diary and a lot of luck," Professor Alcorn answered.

"Whose diary?"

"Hold on to your hat, Warden. The diary belongs to Augustus Humboldt, Deke's great-great-great-great-grandfather. There may be another great in there, but you get the gist. We found it in the university's archives for Blair County."

"What does he have to say about Penelope?"

"He didn't believe she was a witch. The three women who accused her did it out of jealousy and spite. Penelope was marrying the most popular eligible bachelor in Blair County and one of the women thought that should have been her privilege."

"So she's not a witch at all?"

"Can't be sure, but what she is for sure is an angry and terribly wronged spirit. She's still, witch or not, dangerous, Warden Cain."

"Did Deke know about this diary?"

"No, he didn't. This thing was buried under a ton of other journals and artifacts."

"Was Augustus one of the murderers?"

"Yes, he was. He was forced to take part in the killing by his own wife. She was the aunt of the woman who had the vendetta against Penelope. It was a very interesting read."

"Does he say where the bones will be?"

"Yes. At the base of an elm, under a pile of rocks."

"Rita, I hate to be the bearer of bad news, but there are millions of elms in the forests surrounding Canoe Creek. And there are a fair many rocks too."

"So true, Jeremy, but this elm and pile of rocks are next to the western bank of Canoe Creek at the fork with New Creek."

"Okay then. That sounds a little better, but you know, over time the actual banks may have shifted a bit. Your bones could be under water or washed away."

"Jeremy, if I thought like that, I'd never try at all. Is that what you want?"

"Of course not. I'll think more positively. When you and your team go out there, I hope there's a big neon sign that says *Bones Here* with a big flashing arrow."

"That's the spirit, Jeremy. And obviously you helped the state reach their quota of smart asses the year you were hired."

They both laughed and began to fall into a comfortable friendship. For a ghost chaser, Rita was a decent woman. And as a professor, she had a warmer personality and was more approachable than what he expected.

They said their goodbyes and he hung up the phone. Everything was falling into place. Tomorrow would be the big day that Doctor Slocum publicly announces his discovery.

The world will change tomorrow morning, he thought.

Doctor Slocum had not slept all night. He was finalizing every test he could think of that could solidify his body of evidence for a new species.

The thing was seven foot, eleven and one-half inches tall as a dead specimen. In life and completely raised up it would have been over eight feet. The corpse weighed five hundred and thirty-one pounds.

Its hands and feet were two to three times the size of its human counterparts. The heart weighed sixteen pounds and was almost the size of a football.

The creature had extremely low body fat and was muscled beyond belief. Its teeth were similar to human teeth. He presumed it was omnivorous. Unfortunately its stomach was empty. It had not eaten in at least the last two days.

It had a hip wound which was severely infected and would have possibly caused its death in the future. He had picked out buckshot from that wound, which confirmed that it was the owner of the chunk of flesh they had been studying.

The most disturbing aspect of the creature was its face. He had always assumed Bigfoot would have an eerily similar face to a human being, only hairier. Instead, he found the face to be almost devoid of hair. Its skin was an almost shiny, leathery black. Like the color of polished ebony.

Its nose was more flat like many species of apes. The ears were not much more than fur covered mounds on either side of its head with a quarter size auditory opening. Slocum couldn't wait to begin dissecting this specimen in earnest. All he had done so far was akin to an autopsy.

His press conference was in two hours. He needed to head home and clean up. This was the day he had dreamed about for so long. The day where he raised an academic middle finger to all the naysayers and mean spirited assholes that drove him underground and eastward.

Ellie arrived at the office a few minutes late. She was the bearer of two cups of Dunkin Donuts coffee and several long johns. They were Jeremy's favorite.

He greeted her with a kiss and a question, "Did I pass muster?"

"I don't know. When I tucked Joshua in, I asked him, 'what do you think of Jeremy?' He replied, 'who?' I followed up with, 'the man that Mommy works with.' And he asks, 'is he going to be my new Daddy?'"

"And what did you say?"

"I said, 'we'll see.' And then I had to drive home. It was late and his grandparents wanted to go to bed."

"We'll see?"

"Yes. What's wrong with that?"

"Very noncommittal on your part," he said with a smile.

"Well, last time I looked at these long beautiful fingers of mine, there wasn't an engagement ring on them.

Ten fingers and not one ring. So, 'we'll see' seemed like a prudent answer."

The phone rang and Ellie picked it up.

"Jeremy, it's Warden Doreemer. She says it's urgent."

Cain picked up the phone quickly and began listening.

After saying, *uh huh* and *I see* several times, he said, "send him down here. I'll take his statement." And then he hung up.

"If you don't mind me asking, what was that about?"

"Doreemer has Clearfield County. She was flagged down by a guy in a beat up truck camper. He had been in Rothrock and was heading home after being attacked," he explained.

"I'm afraid to ask, but attacked by what?" she questioned reluctantly.

"A bear and a mountain lion. Both, together, were trying to break into his camper. And guess who was cheering them on? A screaming woman in a light colored gown. He toughed it out until morning, but his camper barely held together."

An hour and fifteen minutes later a man came walking through the office door looking unhappy and scared.

"You must be Mr. Foster. Have a seat and I'll take your statement."

"I'll give you a damn statement, but who's going to pay for the damage to my truck?"

"Mr. Foster, you have insurance, right?"

"Liability only, Warden. That's it."

"That's unfortunate, but at least you survived. Almost a dozen others didn't."

"What?"

"Haven't you been reading the papers or listening to the local news, Mr. Foster? People have been dying in those woods."

"I don't pay attention to the news. I don't have a television and I don't get the newspaper."

"Mr. Foster, do you live in that truck?"

"Yes. I damn sure do, but now its in shambles."

"I'm sorry you were attacked, but campers, trailers and RVs are prohibited in the park. Only tent camping is allowed." Cain knew that if he had more than one warden in that county Mr. Foster would have found that out a long time ago. He was a squatter and every few years squatters become a nuisance in state and national forests. Of course, he currently didn't have the manpower to do anything about it. And in light of current problems he also didn't care about squatters. They weren't even on his radar.

"I didn't know that," Mr. Foster replied.

From there Mr. Foster gave a detailed account of what happened to him and his truck. It was disturbing. For the second time that Cain knew of Penelope shrieked her way into using the lion and bear combo to attack again.

Lucky for Mr. Foster that he wasn't in a tent. Cain walked outside with Foster and surveyed the damage. Daylight couldn't have come too soon. The camper top was showing serious structural damage. Much more battering would have caused breaches at several points and Foster would have been helpless.

They went back into the building. Ellie came over and whispered something to Jeremy.

Cain asked a question, "Mr. Foster, your family name doesn't ring a bell. I mean, I'm a history buff. And certain names run deep in these parts. Foster isn't one of them. Did your people come from a different part of the state?"

"What in the hell does that have to do with my situation and my ruined truck that nobody's gonna pay for?"

"It has nothing to do with it. I was just curious," Cain lied.

"Let me tell you, sonny boy. My great grandma on my momma's side said it about a thousand times. She'd say, *Dickie, the Kilmartins own this place. We were here first. Don't you ever forget it.*"

Ellie nodded her head and gave a thumbs up. Foster had his back to her.

"Now Kilmartins I've heard of, Mr. Foster. A good family."

"Damn straight. The best, but we've fallen on hard times just like other folks. So, Warden, there isn't any way I can collect on my loss?"

"None, I'm afraid. But I'll tell you what, you can park in Rothrock for a while and I won't run you out."

"Are you nuts? I'm never going in there again."

"I wouldn't try anywhere, Mr. Foster. We've had those same attacks in all the forests around here. You wouldn't be safe anywhere."

"Well thanks for nothing. Now I got to drive over an hour to get home."

"And where is home?"

"None of your beeswax!" And then he stormed out of the office and hopped into his beat up truck.

After Foster pulled out, Ellie asked, "why did you offer to let him stay in Rothrock again. That would be suicide."

"Because I knew he wouldn't do it. The whole time that man was telling his story he was ready to jump out of his skin. I found him to be so offensive that I wanted to see him squirm."

"Oh my gosh! You are mean as a snake. And up to now you've presented yourself as a Boy Scout," she declared with a smile.

"I was a Boy Scout. I was the meanest kid in the troop. While the other kids on a camping trip were out earning their badges, I was looking for frogs and toads to put in their sleeping bags. In fact, one kid I didn't like got a sleeping bag full of poison ivy."

"You couldn't have made Eagle Scout," she challenged.

"I did. I hid in some bushes and took pictures of my Scout leader with his mistress. Then I blackmailed him into giving me Eagle Scout. My parents were so proud."

"Warden Cain, you are full of more crap than the forest picnic area restrooms."

Jeremy busted up and Ellie joined in. "You had me going for a moment."

He looked at her and said, "I just wanted you to know what kind of man you're getting."

"And once again, ten beautiful fingers and no ring. So don't draw too many conclusions," she said holding up her hands for inspection.

That night they went for a pizza and a movie. It was a scifi movie about a derelict spacecraft that was haunted and had space critters on board. Jeremy loved it. Ellie enjoyed it because she loved being with Jeremy.

The last thing he said to her before dropping her off at her place was, "yep, you're right. Those beautiful fingers look awfully plain with no rings on them."

Then he walked back to his car before she could respond.

Chapter 23

All Hell Breaks Loose

When Jeremy pulled into his space, he was greeted by a full parking lot. More than a dozen people were standing on the office porch. He was afraid to open his door. He had conveniently forgotten Slocum's afternoon press conference.

He got out of his car.

"Is it true, Warden? Did you have a Bigfoot at Rothrock State Forest?"

"Warden Cain, when did you know that the murderous beast was Bigfoot?

"Is it true your best friend sacrificed his own life to kill it?

"There's a rumor you have video of it. Can you comment?"

"Why did it take you so long to figure this out?"

"For the record, Warden. How many people did it kill?"

"Is it true you are missing some victim's body parts?"

"How many more of the beasts are out there? And what are you going to do about them?"

"Warden Cain, are all the forests unsafe, or just Rothrock?"

Ellie pulled in and there was nowhere to park. She made a space along the edge of the lot. She saw Jeremy completely surrounded. She didn't know what to do, so she stayed put.

Jeremy climbed the steps to the porch. He waved his arms for silence. He asked everyone to get off the porch and stand in front of him so he could address them all.

Reluctantly they complied.

"Ladies and gentlemen, I heard each of your questions and I will answer you. If you shout and cut me off, you will get nothing."

"We recovered a Bigfoot that was shot and killed by my friend and outdoorsman Deacon Humboldt. He died during the altercation.

"As to there being others, logic would lead an intelligent individual to say yes. The beast had to have been the product of at least one mating pair and there could have been siblings.

"We could only confirm such a creature existed from video that we…," he was cut off.

"Warden Cain, when will you release the video?" asked a red faced portly reporter from only God knows where.

"And now because this asshole broke my rules, I have nothing more to say." He turned, unlocked the office door, stepped inside and relocked it.

Ellie called Jeremy on the office phone and told him she was making a run for the back door. When she got there she had a man and woman stumbling right behind her asking, "Miss, do you work here?"

He opened the door enough for her to pass through, then slammed it shut. "Ha. I knew I could make it!" Ellie yelled.

"Maybe you should have stayed home. This is going to be a mess."

"What did you say to those people? They're calling you every name in the book and I only heard them as I ran by."

"I told them to go to hell. That won't play well in Harrisburg, but that's tough. I knew Slocum's news was going to start a shit storm. Pardon my French."

"Actually, that word has its origins in Germany," she corrected.

"Really? This is how you decide to be helpful?"

She smiled and said, "I never said I wanted to be helpful. This was supposed to be a nice quiet fall and winter internship. But instead, you throw in a pissed off, homicidal ghost and a creature that has only been a myth, until now."

"Ellie, all kidding aside, I'm at a loss as to how to handle these people. I'm a warden, not a PR expert."

"Jeremy, I am not a PR expert either, but I'm pretty sure you're not supposed to tell the press to go to hell."

"I didn't actually say, *Go to hell*. I called one of them an asshole and I refused to talk to them any more."

"Oh, that's much better," she said rolling her eyes. "Do you trust me?"

"Yeah, why?"

"Let me go out there and fill them in. It can't hurt. Bring me up to speed and I'll smooth things over."

Jeremy agreed to the idea and spent the next half hour making sure Ellie knew what he knew, that she didn't mention Penelope and she didn't admit their knowledge of Bigfoot prior to the video.

Ellie stepped out onto the porch. Immediately the barrage started and Ellie whipped out a whistle from nowhere, blew it and silenced them.

She warned them they had already blown one opportunity and the rules hadn't changed. She assured them that she knew what they wanted to know and she would share all the facts as she knew them.

Cain watched out the window as Ellie masterfully recounted all the facts. She was mesmerizing and the press ate it up. When she was finished, she simply told the assembly that if they would raise their hand, she would try to answer any additional questions.

The portly red-faced reporter whom Cain had labeled an asshole raised his hand first. Ellie called on him.

He said, "you've been wonderful. Are all Wardens inept at handling the press themselves?"

The group got quiet after a couple of snorts and chuckles.

Ellie spoke. "The Wardens are tasked with policing the State Forests alone. They are under-manned and out-gunned, as a recent article pointed out. And we just lost Warden Sorenson to poachers. That man looking out the window led the search team to find him and his killers and made the arrests of those very same individuals.

"In addition, they must be experienced at identifying wildlife and all threats that face the creatures. Maintaining the health of the forest also requires they be familiar with all tree and plant species.

"The Wardens also must be up to date on the regulations and laws concerning State Forests, State Game Lands and conservation habitats. So you must excuse them for not taking public speaking courses on top of everything else."

The red-faced jerk looked like he wanted to crawl under a rock. A few of his colleagues applauded Ellie's defense of the wardens.

Ellie said *thank you* to the group and went back inside the office. She smiled at Jeremy who was beaming with pride and awe at the woman who was soon going to be wearing a ring on one of those beautiful fingers.

She said, "what's the matter? Lion mountain got your tongue?"

"Holy crap, Ellie. That was so impressive, I don't know what to say. What the hell?"

"I was president of the debate team in high school. I won several awards. I was good at it. I joined a debate team in college before I had to quit."

"Why did you have to quit?"

"My dad got cancer and my mom needed my help. My little brothers needed my help as well. Family is important to me."

"That explains why you're the oldest intern that they have ever sent me."

"Excuse me, Warden Cain!" she said with a feigned, angry look playing across her pretty face.

"Well, you have to admit that you're a little long in the tooth for a college girl." He quickly ducked as a local yellow pages whizzed past his head.

"Calm down. I take it back. You have the throwing arm of an eighteen year old."

"Warden Cain, you may defend yourself from now on."

"Oh no, lady. You're now the official office Public Relations Director."

"I'm sure that must come with a raise, since it sounds so much more important than elderly college intern," she pressed.

"How about this?" He produced a ring box from his desk drawer.

"He opened the box as Ellie kept saying, "oh my God! Oh my God! Oh my God!"

He pulled out two folded up ten dollar bills and said, "lunch is on me. How about that?"

She began to tear up.

Cain was clueless as to why. "What's wrong? I can't really increase your compensation. I don't have the authority."

In a broken voice she said, "you are an asshole." She then sat down at her desk with her back to him.

He looked at the ten dollar bills and then the jewelry box. *Oh shit,* he thought.

"Ellie, I didn't realize how this looked. When did you possibly think I would have had the time to go get a ring?"

"Just forget it, Warden Cain."

"Warden Cain? Come on, honey. I am getting you a ring as soon as I have time."

"I said forget it, Warden Cain."

He stood behind her scratching his head wondering how he had screwed things up in the blink of an eye.

The phone rang. Ellie was still sniffing and blotting her nose with a Kleenex. Cain picked it up.

"Sir, this is Salas. I'm at Rothrock because some asshole in a Bigfoot costume just got himself shot."

"How bad?"

"Grazed his shoulder."

"Why was he out there in the first place?"

"He said he would rather people shot at him instead of that beautiful majestic creature."

"Well, he got what he wanted, didn't he? What do you need from me?"

"What do you want me to do, sir?"

"Is an ambulance on the way?"

"Yessir."

"Do you have the shooter?"

"Yessir."

"Get his info and confiscate his weapon as evidence if we need it. Oh, and it's not hunting season, so fine him. After you have the gun, let him go."

"Yessir. Just so you know, the forest is full of hunters. All of them are looking for Bigfoot. Should I fine all of them?"

"No. It's no crime to take your rifle for a walk. If they fire at something, then they are hunting out of season and you can fine them."

"What if they say their practicing?"

"Tell them State Forests are posted as illegal areas for target practice and you're practicing ticket writing. I'll be sending Doreemer and Smith to join you, so don't take on any groups until your backup arrives. Anything else?"

"Nope. Thank you, sir."

The conversation was over and he turned to find Ellie on the other line. He went to the restroom and then came back to his desk.

"Ellie, could you call…"

She cut him off, "Smith and Doreemer and send them to Salas. Already done."

"Good. We have some free time. Come with me please." He walked out the front door, she followed. The reporters were mostly gone. Those left were too involved in their own conversations to care about them.

They got into his SUV. He started it up and began to drive. Fifteen minutes later he pulled into a strip mall and parked the car. Ellie had not said a word.

"If you would," he said, and then left the vehicle and once again she followed.

She suddenly realized what he was doing. They were headed towards Baner's Jewelry. She stopped and said, "wait!"

"What now?"

"Don't buy me a ring because I reacted badly back there or because I cried. I don't want it like this."

"You're wrong, Ellie. I am buying you a ring because I love you. I want you to marry me. I want to be a father to Joshua and this is the first free time I've been able to make in a while.

"Plus, I have no idea what you want. So this is my best idea where this is concerned. You go in there and fall in love with a ring or a set of rings. I'll buy them and then, hopefully, we can have sex," he said with a big grin.

"I love you, Jeremy."

"Of course you do. I'm buying you a ring."

She wrapped her arms around his neck and kissed him. They completed their walk to the jewelry store and went inside.

As they were choosing the rings, another man was shot accidentally. Apparently Bigfoot hunters have very low IQs.

Chapter 24

Rita And The Search

The next day, after a very satisfying evening of lovemaking, Cain headed into the office. While en-route he received a phone call from Professor Alcorn.

He re-routed himself. The point where Canoe and New Creeks converge was not that far away. He arrived at Canoe Creek Park ten minutes later. He parked his vehicle and hiked into the forest.

He saw a group of people ahead working with rakes and shovels. Rita was standing giving orders to her troops. She saw him. "Hey Jeremy. So nice of you to join us."

"My pleasure," he said. "Did you find something of interest?"

"Oh, you better believe it. But not yet what we were hoping for," she said coyly.

"Then what?" he replied, trying not to lose his patience. He had a full day ahead of him. He needed to follow up at Rothrock in person and show his support in the midst of a lousy situation. He also wanted to tell Salas about Mr. Foster.

"We have found an area here that is like an animal graveyard: possum, skunks, raccoons, rabbits, fox, squirrels, dogs and at least one feral pig. Skeletons everywhere."

"Do you mean like someone ate them and discarded the bones or what? I'm confused."

"No, Jeremy. These skeletons are mostly intact. It's like the animals were drawn here to die. And even more weird, the other forest animals left the remains alone. No scavengers or predators, nothing has disturbed the area. And we're finding hundreds under the leaves and scrub vegetation."

"That's weird, I'll admit. What's your theory?"

"It's a little weird, but I think Penelope was feeding on their energy. Kind of like a vampire, only she wasn't touching them. She was just zapping their lifeforce. I know it's kind of Stephen King territory, but I believe her remains are right here, somewhere under our feet."

He wasn't sure what to say, but he didn't want to quench her enthusiasm. So he said something encouraging. "I think you're getting close, Rita. The sooner you find her, the better. We had another attack, but luckily the guy lived."

"Well then I should stop talking. In theory, if we map out these skeletons, she should be in the center. See you Jeremy. I'll call when we find her."

"Rita, don't stay out here anytime close to dark."

"We'll be careful."

He turned and began the journey to his office and then on to Rothrock.

Salas, Doreemer and Smith met for coffee at a WaWa near the entrance to Rothrock that they would be using for access to the forest. Their conversation ran along the lines that God filled the world with idiots so that everyone else could do good by helping them navigate life.

Salas shared with them something that Cain had said to him. "He told me he wished nitwits had to wear orange traffic cones on their heads so the rest of us could avoid them." The three laughed heartily at his reference.

Everyone liked Warden Cain, except Muncy. And he of course was gone.

The three Wardens headed to Rothrock for a day of babysitting goofballs with guns. It was almost more dangerous than criminals with guns. At least criminals didn't shoot their own kind.

They talked about putting in for vacation after this Bigfoot crap died down. That was Smith's favorite word, *crap*. He told them he used to say *shit*, but then he married an ex-Mennonite girl and she reformed him. He always got a lot of laughs with that.

They stayed together. It seemed to be the smartest strategy. The Bigfoot hunters were all in groups. Many of the groups were using their hunting time as an excuse to drink beer and tell stories. It truly was a perilous time for the Wardens.

Then they heard the screams followed by gunfire. They ran towards the noise. They saw a man down on the ground, in a clearing, with a badly cut leg. Salas stopped Doreemer just as she was headed to help the man.

To the west side of the clearing were three men with rifles and to the east was a group of four who had taken up defensive positions.

Salas whispered, "these fools are feuding over something." Salas was glad to be holding the Century Arms Catamount Fury II with a five round magazine locked and loaded. He hoped he didn't have to use it for anything other than intimidation.

Two shots rang out from the eastern group. The western clan responded with three. It didn't appear anyone was hit. Thankfully, no one was shooting at the guy on the ground. He was a sitting duck. And that was what convinced Salas that these guys didn't want to kill anybody.

Salas whispered to his two partners, "cover me."

He stood up and walked into the clearing and spoke with confidence, "gentlemen, put down your guns and come out into the open. Do it now."

The east group dropped their weapons and walked towards him. The west tribe had two men coming forward unarmed, but one was holding back and holding onto his rifle.

Smith had a bead on him with his 30.06 and had Salas' back if the guy persisted. Doreemer had moved into the clearing to render first aid to the injured man.

"Come on, pal," Salas said firmly. "Drop it and walk out here like everybody else."

"No. I stabbed that son of a bitch and you're going to try to arrest me. It ain't happening, Ranger."

Before Salas could correct the man's faux pas, Smith took his shot and the man's rifle flew out of his hands and splintered. In the process it also broke three of the man's fingers.

The situation was now successfully under control. An ambulance and the State Police were called. The man was put in restraints, cussing and spitting mad. The warring factions had their rifles confiscated and waited quietly for the police to arrive.

What Salas could ascertain was this: the injured man had tried to steal a small cooler of beer from the other party. He was caught by the man with the broken fingers. He had stabbed him.

Both factions jumped back to defensive positions leaving the wounded guy out in the open to fend for himself. The only problem was that he was cut pretty badly and had to focus on using his own belt to keep from bleeding to death. The State Police would have their hands full.

Cain cleared up the paperwork on his desk and said goodbye to Ellie, gave her a kiss and walked out to head north to Rothrock State Forest. He was unaware of the eventful morning his Wardens had handled. He would be proud of them.

The hour drive was just what he needed to think about what Rita had said. Penelope was amassing a life force from hundreds of animals. It made no sense, but nothing has made sense since the first deaths. Ellie was the only thing keeping him grounded right now. *Thank God,* he thought.

"Doctor Alcorn!" a grad student with a shovel called. "Over here!"

Alcorn ran over. "What do you have?"

"Look, Doctor," he said proudly.

Some large rocks were stacked one on top of the other and next to them was the student's excavation. And there it was, a partially uncovered skull.

Rita dropped to her knees and began scraping with a trowel that she had been using when called over. The skull was being completely unearthed. And then vertebrae, followed by rib bones, arm bones, leg bones and a pelvis. Within an hour they had the complete skeleton of Penelope Sutter.

Rita placed the call to Cain who was being filled in by his wardens about their exciting morning. Cain commended all three for a job well done.

Smith was proud as a peacock. His shot was perfect. He could have just as easily shot the man instead and no one would have blamed him.

Cain offered to take them all to lunch at a nearby Cracker Barrel. They jumped at the chance to be rewarded.

Cain's phone went off.

"Yes, Rita. What is it?"

"We have her, Jeremy. All of her. Penelope is about to be stopped for good."

"That's great, Rita. I'll be tied up the rest of the day at Rothrock. Get her collected and get out of there before dark. Got it?"

"Jeremy, you worry too much. You couldn't pay me enough to stay here after dark. Talk to you tomorrow. I'll let you know what we plan to do."

In less than an hour the bones were gently packed for transport. Her team headed out after a job well done.

Rita couldn't believe their good luck. Without the Humboldt diary, they never would have had a chance to find the remains. Now It was time for the second part of the plan. She prayed that it would work, but she feared God may not be listening.

Chapter 25

Rita And The Grave Site Experience

Rita sat in Cain's office with two of her paranormal colleagues. The one guy looked like Ozzy Osbourne and the other man looked a little like Anthony Hopkins.

Cain knew this may be the most entertaining day of his life. And since this case was breaking new ground at every turn, he decided to go with the flow.

Rita was getting ready to explain the plan. He had to suppress the urge to laugh because Rita and Anthony Hopkins were looking dead serious, but Ozzy was occupied with picking his nose. Ellie noticed it too and made a face that had him doubling down on trying not to laugh.

"The next steps, Warden Cain, are a bit bizarre. But I am assured by my colleagues the steps are accurate according to the corroboration of three ancient texts," Rita began.

Cain cut in, "Are these steps specific to defeating a witch or banishing a ghost?"

"We don't believe she was a witch. The fact that this is two hundred years after her murder is, we believe, coincidence. There are no other stories, beyond her wedding day story, that points any fingers at her being involved in witchcraft.

"So, to answer your question, we are treating her as a malevolent spirit. A ghost, if you will. A very angry, dangerous ghost."

"Okay," he acknowledged. "Please continue."

"We believe her type of spirit is born of innocence lost. A virgin, an innocent, who loses her life, her future, unfairly. From the scant records kept at the time, we have derived that she was between fourteen and sixteen.

"No one among the early settlers had any education to speak of except the priest. His name was Father Frances Goin. He was a Benedictine. He traveled with Pierre-Joseph Didier. When Didier traveled further into Ohio, Goin was left behind to establish Catholicism in the area.

"He would have been the officiant at Penelope's wedding. The Benedictines were right in the mix of the persecutors of witches. He could have stopped those men and women that day, but he didn't. He may secretly have been her accuser."

"Why would the priest accuse a woman of witchcraft secretly? Or at all for that matter?" Ellie asked.

"Because priests were lonely, horny men. And time after time the most beautiful and choicest female members of their community were out of their reach. It was more common than historians care to let on that some priests developed crushes and decided if they couldn't have the object of their desire, then no one would. They simply made accusations through others that the girl was a witch."

"Did they ever try to make advances on the girls they liked?" Ellie followed up.

"Yes. Probably more often than not. And unsuccessfully most of the time. That enabled them to justify being so spiteful. Being spurned is no fun."

"Let me get this straight, from very little to no evidence, you have concocted a whole story-line blaming the priest?" Cain asked.

"Nope," Rita replied. "We actually have taken our cue from Augustus Humboldt. He alluded to the whole thing in his journal. Apparently he didn't like the priest and suspected the priest of pitting his niece against Penelope because he knew of her crush on Penelope's fiancee. The jealousy was already in place and Augustus figured the priest gave it running room."

"It's like a soap opera," Ellie laughed.

Cain spoke again, "I'm with you on the motivations, but what are the steps to put Penelope away? We haven't gotten to that yet."

"We have to find a lamb without blemish. Slit its throat, thoroughly soaking the bones with its blood. Then rebury the bones in the original spot.

"Once the bones are reburied, we must have a consecration service over the grave. The service will help her spirit pass on to the next plain or stage of existence. Then we wait three days and cover the gravesite with ashes from a dogwood tree."

"Why a dogwood?" Cain asked.

"It is a sacred tree. For some Native American groups it is a tree of protection and safety. It has spiritual meaning to the spirit world," Rita answered.

"If she has passed on, why must we cover her grave with ashes?" Ellie wondered aloud.

Rita answered that too. "The ashes will keep her down, in case her spirit doesn't wish to cooperate. It's supposed to keep her in the ground, if you will."

Cain had one last question, "What do we do if this doesn't work? What is Plan B?"

"My dear Warden Cain. There is no Plan B. Either this works or Penelope gets to rule the forest, based upon her own criteria for maiming and killing innocent people."

"I don't think Harrisburg will approve that second option. In fact, I'm sure of it."

After a little smalltalk, Rita and Jeremy set a time for doing what was needed. In two days, at ten in the morning, they would meet at the burial site with a Catholic priest in tow that Rita knew.

In the meantime, Rita's partners, Anthony Hopkins and Ozzy Osbourne, would locate wood from a dogwood tree and create a fair amount of ash. They all would be praying that the ritual works.

Over the next two days arrests were increasing at Rothrock. Most of the infractions involved liquor, littering, the reckless discharge of firearms, public drunkenness and public urination, which usually went right along with the public drunkenness. Salas, Doreemer and Smith worked together like a well oiled machine in keeping each other safe and protected.

The Bigfoot mania was just getting started. Several vendors were arrested for selling Bigfoot souvenirs on State land. Salas and the other Wardens couldn't get over the inventiveness of the souvenir sellers.

You could buy what was billed as an authentic Bigfoot tooth in a bottle, Bigfoot pheromone bait which was actually re-labeled doe urine spray and a Bigfoot hair bracelet. Lie upon lie was being gobbled up by the public.

T-shirts, key rings, mugs, hairy slippers and *I Love Bigfoot* bumper stickers were showing up everywhere. The Wardens agreed they were in the wrong business.

And just in the last day or so, the representatives of the legitimate science community were making an appearance in small teams. Salas could tell them from the others by their LL Bean clothing, their well groomed appearance and their lack of firearms.

They also tended to carry cases full of electronic equipment. What type of gear they brought was lost on Salas and his partners, but they appeared very professional. And there also seemed to be an absence of beer in their midst as well. For which the Wardens were grateful, considering the rest of the forest occupants drinking habits.

The two days passed quickly as the relationship between Jeremy and Ellie grew stronger. Joshua joined them for a day of fun at a local indoor amusement center.

Cain couldn't get over how much fun laser tag was. Ellie enjoyed the miniature golf and Joshua enjoyed everything. The little boy was entering Cain's heart in a big way. He couldn't wait to be his stepfather. Cain knew that was not normal for most men to be so smitten by another man's child, but it was happening and he was glad. It made his love for Ellie so complete. His years without a family would soon be over.

Ellie had similar thoughts. She couldn't believe her good fortune to find a man like Cain. She thought, *how can I go from worst to first in the husband department.* She promised herself she wouldn't dwell on her blessings too much for fear of jinxing them.

The happy trio enjoyed the day. Tough times were coming. They didn't know how tough. They would soon find out what limits they could endure.

The morning of their ritual came quickly. Ozzy and Anthony were there. They told Rita they had the ashes ready for the second part of the ceremony three days from now.

Cain had asked Salas to join them. He made the introductions and everyone was very cordial. This was Cain's way of keeping Salas in the loop. He had already been indoctrinated into the strangeness of the whole situation.

She seemed pleased and then she introduced Father Mulcahey to the group. Cain smiled and opened his mouth, but was cut off by the priest. "Please, no M*A*S*H jokes. It was tough enough being a kid with that name, but after becoming a priest, the floodgates really opened.

"I don't know Alan Alda or Loretta Swit. I've never served in the military or ridden in a helicopter or been to Korea. Does that about cover it?"

"You're not a surgeon?" Cain asked facetiously.

"I'm afraid, Warden Cain, I can't even fix a boo-boo, unless it's spiritual. Then I may be able to help. Besides, the good Father wasn't a surgeon. Just for the record."

"If we're all finished with our levity, let's get down to business," Rita insisted.

A grad student dug at the original site where the bones were unearthed. He made the hole longer and deeper. It was roughly rectangular, as would be befitting a coffin.

Rita unpacked the bones and laid them in the hole starting at one end with the skull and then working her way down to the feet. She was very gentle and reverent as she proceeded.

Once the bones had been ceremoniously laid out, the grad student covered them with spade after spade of dark, rich-looking dirt. When finished, he nodded to Rita.

"Go ahead, Father. It's all yours," she said.

The priest began with a prayer and spoke a typical committal service. Cain was surprised there was no extra mumbo jumbo that would be reminiscent of an exorcism, even though he knew this didn't fit the criteria of possession.

He thought there would at least be something extra to keep that bitch in the ground. He surprised himself by his anger in that moment. The loss he felt recently was still very raw.

After the service was over, Rita asked the grad student to mark the grave by driving a cross into the ground at the head of the grave. That's when things changed.

As soon as the cross was firmly seated in place, they all began to smell a sulphureous odor. Little dirt devils kicked up and spun the dead leaves into swirls all around them.

The air became demonstrably colder as it blew around them. And Cain saw movement in the darkness at the forest edge, but when he quickly looked in that direction there was nothing discernible. He could hear Salas say, "what the fuh…"

Just as quickly as the change came upon them it ceased. It warmed a bit, the dirt devils disappeared and the air took on the sweet smell of autumn leaf decay with a slight tinge of wood fire smoke, which Cain loved so much.

The group looked at each other perplexed as to what they had collectively experienced. Anthony Hopkins asked, "you sure we have to wait three days to seal her in with the ash? I vote we do it now."

"No, Carl, that won't work. There is something to being three days in the earth like Christ was. It shows up in several cultures as a death rite. We wait three days, no less," Rita declared emphatically.

The last thing Cain saw as they left was Ozzy picking his nose again. He wondered to himself, *where did she get these guys?*

Chapter 26

An Unexpected Twist

Early in the morning the next day, while Jeremy and Ellie were in the office working on the monthly Warden's report, the phone rang. Ellie answered.

"Jeremy, you better take this. The guy sounds frantic. Line one." It was the only line lit, but she had gotten used to always identifying the line that needed his attention. For such a small office, they received a fair amount of calls.

The first thing she heard that drew her attention was Jeremy's response to what he was being told.

"You must be kidding," pause. "Yes, I know you wouldn't kid about that, but it's unbelievable. What are the police calling it?" pause, "What do you think?" pause. "Has anybody checked on Mulcahy?" pause. "Let me know," he ended.

"Jeremy, what is it?"

"Rita Alcorn is dead. She fell down a flight of stairs going to her basement. Broke her neck."

"Oh my. Poor woman. I take it she lives alone?"

"Yes, honey, she lives alone. But if I were a betting man, I'd bet she wasn't alone when she fell."

"What are you saying?"

"Geez, think about it. We re-bury Penelope's bones yesterday and begin the process of shutting her down and the person in charge of that ends up dead."

"So you really do believe in Deke's witch completely now, don't you?"

"Yes. Yesterday's little dust up convinced me. I'm telling you, Ellie, it got ice box cold instantly and those little tornado things sprang up all around us. And I saw something in the woods. Oh yeah, the smell of fire and brimstone was pretty convincing too."

She giggled. "Fire and brimstone? I thought you said it was sulphur."

"That is what they say fire and brimstone smells like."

She began laughing. He looked at her angrily.

"I'm sorry, Jeremy. I know a woman has died and I shouldn't laugh, but you're starting to sound like Deke."

"Laugh your head off. A woman has indeed died and I think she was murdered. And before you ask," he paused, "yes, by a ghost. So there. You're marrying a kook!"

"Don't be mad. This is freaking me out too. So what's next?"

"I don't know. That was her colleague Thomas on the phone. You know, the Anthony Hopkins look-alike, not booger Osbourne. He's checking up on the priest who did the actual ceremony."

Two hours passed as they discussed what had happened to the group on the previous day. They couldn't find the wherewithal to get back to the reports.

Cain touched base with Salas and his team. Things were good. He also put out feelers to a few other wardens. The reports coming back were not near as crazy as the Rothrock area.

There were some Bigfoot hunters up in Erie, Clarion and Butler, but there had been no nonsense to be concerned about. He needed to touch base with everyone, to make sure they were safe.

He did have a couple of single Wardens who wouldn't have a wife or partner to report them missing if anything happened. That had always concerned him. Damn budget constraints had already gotten Sorenson killed. He should have had a partner.

Several calls had interrupted their conversation and the phone rang once again. This time Jeremy answered.

Ellie saw the look on his face and stood up, walked over and took a position beside him with her hand on his shoulder.

"Thomas, find your partner and that grad student and hold up somewhere for a few days. Call me tonight and let me know where you are." He then hung up and looked at Ellie with a look of fear that she had never seen on his face before.

"Jeremy, what is it?"

"The priest is dead. They found him hanging in the church library."

"He killed himself?"

"I doubt that he did it without coercion."

"From who?"

"Who have we been talking about? Penelope!"

"But how could she? She's just a ghost."

"Honey, we've already seen her controlling Bigfoot, a mountain lion and a bear. Who knows what else she can do? There are four of us left who were there. You need to get out of here for a few days."

"No! I want to be with you. I wasn't there. She shouldn't have a beef with me."

"Ellie, she's already proven that collateral damage is of no concern. I can deal with her better if you're not here."

Suddenly the power went out. It was mid-afternoon with thunderstorms rolling in. It was preternaturally dark for this time of day.

"Jeremy, I just saw someone flit by the window. It was barely perceptible."

"It's her! She's here for me! I can't let anything happen to you. Get out! Get in your car and drive. GO NOW!"

She grabbed her purse and shot out the door as fast as her legs would carry her. Maybe if she didn't have a son to think of she would have stayed, but motherhood dictated not taking that chance. Joshua was first in her life.

She jammed her car in reverse and screeched backwards. Then she snapped it into drive and quickly pulled towards the parking lot exit.

Jeremy watched it all from an office window. Just as Ellie was pulling out of the parking lot, a face appeared in her back window. It was smiling and it wasn't Ellie's face. He knew it was Penelope hitching a ride to do who knows what.

He ran out of the office waving his arms and screaming. It was too late. She was gone.

He ran to his SUV, jumped in and tried to start it. He heard nothing but a clicking noise. He tried again. He got out and looked under his hood. The distributor cap was missing and several wires were melted and scorched.

"How in the hell does a two hundred year old ghost know about cars?" he said aloud.

He reached deep in his pocket and pulled out his cellphone. The battery was completely dead. He had just charged it last night.

Running back into the office he grabbed his land line. No dial tone. He checked all four lines. Dead.

He ran outside to look at the telephone junction box. It was popped open and all the wires were pulled out and melted.

She knows phones too? This is wrong on every level, he thought.

He grabbed his walkie-talkie. It was the one item the state didn't go for cheap. The ones they used were the Uniden GMR5095-2CKHS with a range of fifty miles.

Rothrock was forty miles away. He hoped Salas was listening.

"Warden Salas, this is Warden Cain, over."

He repeated his call three times and finally Salas answered.

He told Salas he couldn't explain, but he needed him to call Diehl's Garage and have Jimmy Diehl come pick him up. It was an emergency. He gave Salas the number and then sat back and waited.

In the meantime he was charging his phone. He was going out of his mind with worry. Eleven minutes later Jimmy Diehl came screeching into the parking lot.

Jimmy jumped out of his truck, pistol in hand and yelled, "what's wrong, Cain?"

"My truck won't start and I think Ellie's in danger!"

"Let me look," Jimmy commanded.

The hood was already up.

"Your distributor is all messed up."

"Jimmy, let me take your truck and you can get one of your boys to pick you up."

"Want me to come with?"

"No. Just please give me the keys."

Jimmy chucked him the keys, no questions asked. Cain had more than earned the respect of the locals.

Cain jumped into the old pickup, slammed the door shut and screeched out of the parking lot. Ellie only lived seven minutes away. He hoped he wasn't too late.

He arrived six minutes later and hopped out. Ellie was at her door and came running towards him.

"Jeremy!" she screamed through frantic tears. "She's got Joshua!"

He came to an abrupt halt as he ran towards her. The words were a hard slap and yet he was having trouble processing them.

"Jeremy, did you hear me? She's got my baby! Joshua's gone!"

"I heard you, but how? She's a fricking ghost, not a kidnapper. I mean, how could she physically take him?"

"She used the boy next door. He has autism. He came out after I parked. The babysitter was bringing Joshua out to greet me. The neighbor kid came out and grabbed him and started running.

"I caught up, but he turned and knocked me down. Mrs. Jiminez, the babysitter, called the police. They should be here any minute."

"Which way did the kid go?"

She pointed east towards the woods.

"That damn broad loves trees, doesn't she?" he said as he began sprinting towards the woods' edge.

A siren could be heard in the distance as Cain entered the woods that was part of the Canoe Creek State Park. Visibility in the forest was difficult because of the overcast conditions. There were no rays of sunlight or sun dappled forest floor. Gloom permeated the entire area.

Cain felt himself begin to feel out of his element. He knew these woods well, but today they felt foreign and threatening. The lack of light was disorienting.

About twenty yards into the woods he came to a halt and just listened. He heard a child call out *Mommy*. It was Joshua, he had no doubt. Unfortunately, it was too faint to get a bead on the direction. He listened even more intently.

He heard a crashing sound like a large body moving through thick brush. That was followed by a yelp of pain. It was ahead and to the left. Cain began sprinting in that direction, in as much as one could sprint while leaping over logs, twigs, roots and short bushes that filled the forest at ground level.

The sounds ahead of him were getting louder.

He came to a clearing. There stood the neighbor kid, holding on tightly to Joshua. Ellie's son looked at Cain with eyes big as saucers. The poor child had no idea that the world was a dangerous place, until now. Cain hoped it wouldn't scar him for life.

"What's your name, big boy?" Cain said to Penelope's puppet.

Most people with autism don't even warrant a second look. Many show no signs in calm circumstances or short windows of observation, but this kid was different. His condition must have been more severe, for he had the look of the mildly deranged. The crazy darting eyes, disheveled hair, the constant grin, as if the world were a laughable place all the time. Cain counted himself as extremely worried in regards to reasoning with this overgrown child.

The boy was large. Cain couldn't gauge his age, but guessed he might be thirteen or fourteen, but looking the size of a twenty year old. Not muscled, but oafishly strong he was sure. Strong enough to hurt Joshua and he couldn't allow that to happen.

"Come on, big boy. Give me your name so we can talk."

The boy stared maniacally his way. The grin still plastered on his face and drool collecting at the corners of his mouth.

"His name is Peter!" Joshua yelled.

"Okay, Pete. Why don't you let Joshua go?"

"He doesn't like Pete. Call him Peter," Joshua corrected.

"Peter is a great name. How about letting our little buddy Joshua go now. Okay?"

"She wants you to suffer," Peter said very clearly, which surprised Cain considering how the boy looked.

Cain could hear distant voices coming from the woods. The police had finally arrived. He hoped they wouldn't scare Peter and force him to act rashly. Of course, if Penelope were still in control rationality was out the window.

"Can you talk to her?" asked Cain.

The boy wailed piteously. "She's in my head. Make her leave me alone."

Cain came up with an idea. "Peter, if you let Joshua go, she'll leave. I promise."

Without a moments' delay, Peter pushed Joshua away from himself. Joshua ran towards Cain and Cain ran forward to grab him before Penelope could regroup. It didn't take long.

Peter screamed and lunged forward intent on murder. Cain pushed Joshua behind him and steeled himself for the onslaught. Just as Peter reached him, two policemen ran past Cain and wrestled Peter to the ground. He was quite a handful, but a third cop jumped in and they cuffed him.

Looking up from the ground with hate-filled eyes, Peter let out a string of obscenities that would have made a longshoreman blush. The boy's eyes were boring through him and he knew he was looking into Penelope's rage.

Within two minutes Peter was quiet, docile and completely confused as to how he ended up on the ground in cuffs. She was gone.

Ellie ran to Joshua. He was safe. The first thing he asked his mom was, "can we have Burger King for supper?"

Amazing, Cain thought. *This could have been the kid's swan song and all he knows is that he's hungry and he can use the situation to get a burger for supper.* Cain just shook his head.

His next thought was, *will she try to get at me again?* He knew the answer. His biggest concern was that Penelope knew that Ellie and Joshua were part of his life equation.

In one more day they could lay down the ash. Penelope was obviously scared of that. Maybe that's where the next showdown would take place. Of course, his mood became dark. Cain wasn't ready to rumble with bears and mountain lions.

A flash followed by a peal of thunder announced the rain. It began to fall in big drops. Everyone ran for cover and continued through the woods to their cars.

Ellie, Joshua and Jeremy went back to Ellie's place where a police officer took statements from all three. When he was satisfied, he told them he would be in touch and took his leave.

"I need to go back to the office and lock up. I also need to make some calls. When I'm finished, I'll be back with a bag. I'm sleeping here on the couch tonight. It's necessary."

"I agree Jeremy," then she leaned forward and whispered, "maybe you can pay a visit to my bedroom after someone falls asleep."

"If you make it worth my while," he laughed.

"I have chocolate in there," she smiled.

"It's a date. Now I have to go return a truck and see if my SUV is drivable. And then onto the office."

Chapter 27

A Showdown

The evening had gone as well as they had hoped. They played games together, laughed and ate popcorn. Joshua didn't even talk about the day's incident with Peter. It was already behind him.

He never got his Burger King meal, but Ellie made fried chicken, mashed potatoes and chocolate cake, which was his favorite meal. He went off to bed at seven o'clock with nary a peep. The rest of the evening Cain spent telling Ellie what had transpired since he left them after Joshua's rescue.

His narrative detailed returning Jimmy Diehl's truck and finding Jimmy working on his SUV. Shortly after finding Jimmy at work, his vehicle was ready to go. And where he went next was his office.

At the office he arranged for Salas, Smith and Doreemer to be present at the ash scattering, which was supposed to be the last step in locking Penelope into the ground for good.

He told her that he wanted the other Wardens present for the additional firepower, in case Penelope threw a herd of wild animals at them. Each Warden would be packing a shotgun. None of the three really understood what was going on, but they trusted Cain, and that was enough.

After charging his cellphone, he called Anthony Hopkins and Booger Osbourne. At this point Ellie broke in, "what are their real names? You can't keep calling them Anthony Hopkins and Booger Osbourne."

"I don't remember. The Hopkins look-alike's name was Carl and I have his phone number. I can't remember his last name. And Booger, well, I don't remember his first or his last. And to be honest, I really like the name Booger Osbourne."

She shook her head, rolled her eyes and said, "oh, brother. What kind of man am I getting involved with? Just continue."

He explained that tomorrow at noon, four Wardens, Carl and Booger, and three grad students would finish the ceremony or rite. They would spread the ashes, say a prayer over the remains and then hope for the best.

"Who gets to say the prayer? It should be someone with a strong faith. I know you go to church sometimes, but you had a priest before and now he's dead."

"Well that's the funniest part, Ellie. Booger is an ordained Baptist preacher. Pastor Booger. It has a nice ring to it," he joked.

"How can you be so jovial at a time like this? Tomorrow you may be going toe to toe with the meanest dead bitch that ever... well I guess *lived* isn't the right way to end that. But you know what I mean. Jeremy, I'm scared for you."

"Ellie, I'm plenty scared, but this has to be done or more people will continue to be killed. And remember, she's still after the rest of us. Remember Rita, Father Mulcahey and she went after Joshua to get at me. Not one of us is safe until she's put down."

"Then since tonight's lovemaking may be our last, we better make it good," she said with a teasing smile playing across her lips.

"Well, thanks for putting it that way. My balls just shriveled up."

"Don't worry. I'll get them ready and raring to go."

With that, they retired to the bedroom to unleash their love and passion for one another. They both knew that their time could be running out.

The next morning, at around ten-thirty, the spiritual combatants met at Cain's office. Cain had decided to level with his Wardens so that they may be prepared for anything.

Salas was on board from word one. He had been privy to most of what was going on. Smith and Doreemer were not far behind. They knew weird shit was happening just by the series of events that led up to finding the dead Bigfoot. Their belief system was becoming larger by the minute.

Doreemer was a devout Catholic. She admitted that she thought the exorcism stuff that the church became noted for was a farce, until now. She was open to a broader spectrum of spiritualism than she had ever imagined.

Smith was an agnostic. He believed in a higher power, but he called her Mother Nature. He had Susquehanna in his lineage, so believing in a Great Spirit was really part of his DNA. He apologized to Doreemer for not being able to believe in the whole Jesus thing, as he put it.

The grad students stayed quiet during the entire conversation. Cain asked them their thoughts. The three remained very noncommittal as to their beliefs. They just expressed their eagerness to carry on Rita's work.

Booger expressed his apprehension as to his current qualifications as an ordained minister. He hadn't even been to church for years, he explained. His faith hadn't lapsed, but his confidence in organized religion had taken a hit years ago after a woman in his church accused him of inappropriate relations with her daughter.

He provided that the relationship was a friendship that had common ground in a love for birdwatching. Unfortunately, on one of their outings the young woman offered herself to him and he spurned her affections. The accusation came shortly thereafter. The church threw him under the bus to avoid a drawn-out scandal. His ordination remained in place, but he could never pastor a church again in his denomination.

"Well, that certainly doesn't disqualify you for this mission, Tom." That was his real name. Cain almost called him Booger.

Booger smiled nervously at Cain and said, "so let's get this party started."

The contingent drove to Canoe Creek Park. Carl, Tom and the three grad students in one vehicle and Cain, along with his three Wardens in Cain's SUV. They parked and began preparing their gear.

Booger brought along a crucifix, which was a bit unusual for a Baptist. He also brought his bible. Carl was carrying a ten pound bag of ashes. The grad students carried shovels for spreading the ashes evenly.

The Wardens were much better armed: sidearms, two shotguns and two AR15s. All four of them were unsure what they would face, but they were determined to be ready for anything. That is, anything that they could think of. Penelope had been totally unpredictable thus far.

They banded together and began to walk to the site where the grave marked by the cross was located. It was a peaceful walk in the woods. It was warm for a late fall day.

The group stopped at the edge of the area where they had last worked with Rita and Father Mulcahey. For five out of the eight it was a nostalgic, bittersweet moment. Their two comrades were gone. They hoped there would be no more casualties.

They began to move forward. Cain held out his arms halting the others advance and yelled, "STOP!"

Booger asked, "what's wrong, Ranger?"

"It's Warden, not Ranger and look at the ground."

Everyone looked ahead and downward. The ground was moving. The area around the wooden cross was slowly churning.

Salas was the first to realize what they were looking at.

"Sir, it's snakes! Hundreds, maybe thousands, of snakes covering the ground around that wooden cross. Maybe three or four hundred square feet of twisting, wiggling and roiling snakes."

"Are they poisonous?" asked Carl.

Cain told the group to stay put as he moved forward. He wanted to identify the snakes. He stopped when he heard the first rattle. By then he could see well enough to not only identify rattlesnakes, but also copperheads.

"She's doing her best to stop us," Cain said aloud. He couldn't believe that she had the ability to control snakes, but why not? She had controlled a heretofore mythical creature, a bear and a mountain lion. As the kids say today, *that bitch got skills.*

Booger spoke up, "I think she has succeeded. I'm not walking among a thousand or more poisonous snakes. No fucking way!"

The three grad students concurred.

"How do we clear them out, sir?" Doreemer asked.

"Let me think, guys," requested Cain. He actually thought the situation was hopeless, but wasn't ready to be turned away.

He turned to Salas. "I have a spray pump half-full of weed killer in my vehicle and a two and a half gallon can of gas. Go get them."

Salas was off like a shot. He knew what Cain was thinking and he thought it just might work. Salas knew better than Doreemer or Smith what they were dealing with. He knew how serious the situation was.

While Salas was off on his errand, the grad students became a little more vocal. Heather, a geology master's candidate, seemed to be the most terrified by what lay ahead. She had a snake phobia from childhood and was currently on the border of hysteria.

Cain sized her up and told her to return to the cars and keep an eye on them. "Tell Salas to hurry, Heather. I don't know how long the snakes are willing to stay put."

Heather took off like a shot.

"You think she might need help?" asked James, a biology student.

The group actually laughed at his attempt at humor. At least they thought he was being humorous, but James had a small hope that maybe Cain or the professors would send him to keep an eye on Heather. He had to take his shot.

Salas returned with the items he had been sent to retrieve. Cain grabbed the pump, removed the top and poured the weed killer onto a patch of stones, hoping that that would cause the least amount of harm.

He then unscrewed the top of the gas can and filled the pump. He looked at the group and asked if anyone had a lighter. He knew Booger did because he had seen him smoking earlier.

"Oh, here," Salas was heard saying. "I grabbed two flares from your tire compartment. I almost forgot."

Cain was grateful. They were the perfect tool.

He began pumping and then spraying the gas on the edge of the clearing full of snakes. The pumping was sending a mist at least eighteen feet in any direction it was pointed.

Salas popped the flare and it came to life.

"Let me get out of the way," Cain instructed. Once he was at a safe distance, he yelled, "DO IT!"

Salas threw the flare into the midst of the snakes. Recent rain storms had assured the Wardens that the surrounding forest would be reasonably safe from catching fire.

The area of snakes ignited with a low *whump* sound.

The snakes made no noise, but a quiet crackling could be discerned as the ground became even more active. The snakes were being burnt alive and they gave off an unusual odor. It wasn't offensive, nor was it enticing. It was just a unique and almost musky odor.

The crackling grew a little louder as groundcover became involved. The noise was just enough to cover the crashing and crushing of vegetation as a three hundred and fifty pound black bear emerged from the treeline and made a beeline towards James.

The first to realize the danger was Carl. He pushed James away as the bear lunged. He and the bear went down. All air was knocked from his lungs and he felt the searing pain as the bear bit into his scalp.

A gunshot cracked as Smith withdrew and fired his Browning 9mm. Unfortunately, his bullet hit the mark to no effect and the bear reared up while simultaneously swiping at Carl and damn near obliterating his face.

A shotgun blast moved the bear back. A second blast dropped it. Carl lay on the ground bleeding through scratches on his lower jaw where the bear just narrowly missed removing his head. Doreemer jacked in a third round, but it was unnecessary.

Smith was on his walkie-talkie to the County 911 system, calling for an ambulance. Terry, the third grad student, had jumped away from the bears attack, but had inadvertently moved closer to the roiling snakes. A six foot timber rattler that had evaded the destruction and carnage of the fire took advantage and struck Terry in the ankle. He fell to the ground and screamed and the snake struck again.

Cain grabbed the shovel James had dropped when Carl had pushed him. He raised it up and brought it down, decapitating the rattler. Thank God an ambulance was already enroute.

The ambulance arrived. The group had moved the victims sixty yards closer to where they had parked their vehicles. Even so, the ambulance crew noticed the fire in the clearing. Cain told them it was a controlled burn for fire prevention purposes.

Booger tried to go with Carl in the ambulance. Cain grabbed him. "Booger, you can't go. We need to finish this and he isn't hurt that badly."

"What did you call me?" Tom asked.

"I'm sorry. Sometimes I call people Booger. It's a childhood thing," Cain lied.

Booger stayed. The Wardens stayed. James stayed. They sent Heather in the ambulance with Terry and Carl.

Their nine person team was now down to six. Warden Cain wondered what else Penelope had in store for them. He didn't have to wonder long.

Salas and Doreemer began using shovels to throw charred snakes out of the way. Many were still writhing and twisting as they were being thrown aside. Twenty minutes passed before the area around the grave was cleared.

The wooden cross still stood, though badly charred. Booger prepared to open the ashes they had brought when the group heard low guttural growls coming from the west edge of the clearing.

They turned in unison to see four huge coyotes bearing down on them. Salas dropped his shovel and drew his pistol and fired without hesitation. He had left his AR 15 leaning up against a tree when he picked up the shovel. He missed but the pack halted and stared at their human adversaries.

The hesitation was long enough for Cain and Smith to level their weapons at the creatures. Doreemer drew her pistol. She had handed her shotgun to James earlier, but the kid was clueless as to what to do with it.

Cain fired his shotgun towards the pack, but above them. He didn't want to hurt the animals if he didn't have to. They moved forward. Not the reaction he expected or wanted.

The alpha continued to move forward, growling. Two more coyotes appeared slightly to the east of the original group. Cain wondered how many Penelope could control.

He saw movement to his left. Three more coyotes entered the clearing. This was a FUBAR situation if he ever saw one. Nature was not to be controlled in this way, yet he couldn't deny what he was seeing. These extremely wild animals were being manipulated to become a canine army, of sorts. There were too many.

They were being stared down by nine coyotes. Not the typical skinny thirty-five pound variety that were the most commonly seen. These were strong fifty pound specimens. Each one shared an identical snarl. Canine teeth seemed to dominate their current reality.

It was almost as if Penelope had chosen the alphas from nine different packs, but there were typically only three or four packs in this region. Cain's mind was working overtime to formulate a plan.

Salas was edging towards his rifle, pistol in hand. One of the beasts broke into a run and leaped at James. Impressively, James used the shotgun like a baseball bat and swung away. A sickening crunch could be heard by the group. The coyote went down with a yelp. James went down as well, and as he was falling a second coyote launched itself at him as he scrambled to get up. Too late. The beast had him by the arm and was shaking its huge head trying to cause maximum damage.

Unbelievably, James remained almost silent except for a few grunts and groans in the heat of battle. Doreemer was closest and took the shot. The coyote yelped, rolled and ran off. The men didn't call her *Annie Oakley* for nothing. She was raised with firearms and was an excellent shot. Put most of them to shame, if truth be told.

Two more coyotes were emboldened by their comrades. The first coyote that was struck by James remained down on its side panting. He was no threat currently.

The two spoiling for action moved towards Salas just as he reached his rifle. He clicked the safety off and swung around spewing lead at the fast-approaching pair. One was hit immediately and dropped like a sack of concrete. The second reached to within seven feet of Salas before it was struck and tumbled back.

Five more coyotes to go and Cain shouted, "screw it!" He fired and pumped several rounds at the group of four that were showing evil intent. All four received a few pellets of buckshot and lost their will to pursue the game.

One left. It charged Booger and was on him before any of them could react. Smith was now closest, but was frozen. He didn't want to fire for fear of striking their team member. So he took a page out of James' playbook and used his AR 15 like a club. Bad move.

The canine pushed off of Booger and caught Smith by the neck. Within seconds Smith's throat was gone and Salas shot the wild thing to death. Smith was dead before any of the group could reach him.

Cain radioed for an ambulance and yelled at Booger to spread the damn ashes and say a damn prayer. The coyote threat was gone. The snake danger had been stalled.

They had to act fast before Penelope sent something else after them. He remembered the comment about sending beavers to slap them to death with their tails. It was still funny, but there was no time to laugh.

Booger opened the bag of ashes and covered the grave thoroughly. He then said the Lord's Prayer out loud. He finished and turned to Cain. "Now what?"

"Hell if I know," he said to the Ozzy Osbourne look-alike and he meant it. Without Rita he wasn't sure what to do.

The rest of the afternoon went slowly and sadly. James was packed off into an ambulance with Booger. A coroner's hearse took away a hell of a good man and the remaining three had a mountain of paperwork to file.

Cain called Ellie and explained everything. She offered to come to the office with dinner for the three of them and he accepted gratefully.

The deceased coyotes had to have pieces and parts sent to the lab to check for rabies and other parasites, pests and contagions. Someone would demand an explanation for nine large coyotes attacking six people. Erratic behavior to say the least. Cain wasn't sure how he would explain it.

He knew that once the details emerged in the media, the public would panic and idiots with guns would fill the woods looking for revenge, or their fifteen minutes of fame as a self-appointed hero. Ultimately, those people would be just as dangerous as Penelope.

When they finally reached the office, Ellie greeted them with hugs and a fried chicken meal that was nothing short of spectacular. Salas made the best comment. "Ellie, being scared shitless, pardon my French, and losing my friend Smitty, guaranteed that this was going to be my worst day ever. But somehow this kindness of yours, this fantastic feast, helps take some of the sting away. Thank you.

"If Cain doesn't marry you, I'll ask my wife if we can become Mormons. Then I'll marry you myself."

Laughter, something they thought would be lacking this day, was heard and experienced by all.

"Sorry to tell you this, Warden Salas, but the Mormons don't do that anymore. You'll just have to become a bigamist and hide me away in another town," Ellie joked.

"Okay, listen up. We've all tasted this fried chicken, so you know darn well I'm going to marry the woman," Cain declared. Again laughter filled the room.

They finished eating and began their reports while Ellie cleaned up. Laughter was over for now. Tears were coming. Their loss weighed heavier as the night wore on.

Ellie had been gone for hours. It was now just the three of them. It was after midnight. They were all bone weary.

When Salas, Doreemer and Cain were alone, Salas spoke. "Something kind of bothers me, sir."

"Salas, I know I'm your boss, but please call me Jeremy. We have shared too much work and too much loss to remain so formal."

"Okay, Jeremy. We entered the clearing and immediately we were surprised by the snakes. Even with that happening I knew something seemed off. I thought about it as I returned to your vehicle to get the pump and gas, but forgot about it when I got back and we began cooking the snakes.

"I was going to mention it again, but the damn coyotes showed up and had us all on edge. Losing Smitty had me so defeated that I couldn't think straight to save my life," Salas explained.

"Salas, no offense, but cut to the chase. What's bothering you?"

"Sir... I mean Jeremy, I don't think that cross was in the same place we left it."

Chapter 28

Waste Of Time

Warden Salas went on to explain to Cain and Doreemer that on the day they reburied the bones he remembered thinking to himself that the cross was placed dead center between the creek and a huge elm tree at the edge of the clearing.

It was just a passing thought he had that day and kept to himself. A personal observation similar to many others he makes every day in regards to spatial relationships. It was the way his mind worked.

The bottom line of his observation was that someone moved the cross so that the ashes were put down in the wrong place. In other words, Penelope was still free to carry on her reign of terror.

Cain felt the hair on the back of his neck rise. This meant that they were all still in danger, including Ellie and Joshua. Doreemer was just coming on-board with the reality of the situation. She hadn't been as intimately involved as Cain and Salas.

"So you guys are telling me this shit is real? We are being played by a two hundred year old witch?" she asked incredulously.

"The truth is, she may not be a witch at all. She could just be a two hundred year old, super pissed off spirit. She may have been falsely accused and is back for revenge," Cain explained.

"So this is my life now? Bigfoot and witches, or ghosts, all proven real in like three weeks. It's a little much to process in so short a time. I just have one question I want answered," Doreemer requested.

"Shoot," Cain replied.

"Is Santa Claus real? Cause I may have lied to my kids."

Unbelievably, the three Wardens laughed until they cried. It was just what they needed. Serious business lie ahead. This was their time to relax and let some of the strain be released before facing up to the reality of Salas' revelation.

The next day, Cain called Booger. It didn't go well.

"Tom, this is Warden Cain. We need to talk."

"About what, Warden Cain? We put this thing to rest, right? I just want to get back to teaching my classes and forget this stuff. Carl feels the same way. No more weirdness for a while," he responded.

"Tom, we strongly believe that all this weirdness isn't over. We have reason to believe that Penelope outsmarted us."

There was silence from the other end of the line.

"Tom, are you still there?"

"What do you mean, she outsmarted us? We finished the ritual just like Rita had prescribed."

"My colleague, Warden Salas, noticed that the cross was moved. We laid down the ashes on the wrong area. Bottom line Tom, we accomplished nothing. She is still free to hurt and kill. We need a different plan."

"No, Cain. *You* need a different plan. Me and Carl are done. No more. This shit is too dangerous."

"Tom, she killed Rita and Father Mulcahey. You two are not safe. She may still come after all of us."

More silence.

"Tom, there has to be something we can do. Just tell us and we can try it without you, unless it requires clergy."

"Hell, Cain, I'm not even sure I'm considered clergy any more. I've asked God a million times and he ain't talking. So I doubt if you really need me, but I'll talk to Carl and see if there is another route we can take."

They finished their conversation and Cain felt the need to call Ellie. She was at the office and he had given her permission to bring Joshua with her. He wanted them to be safe and even their trusted babysitter didn't seem like a good idea.

Ellie answered on the third ring. "Hello, Warden Cain's office."

"Warden Cain's a jerk," he said into the phone.

"Couldn't agree more, sir. Thank you for calling." She hung up giggling to herself.

The phone rang again.

"Warden Cain's office."

"You couldn't agree more?"

"You told me to be pleasant and never argumentative. I get calls like that all the time. That's how I handle them," she said smiling broadly.

"You are some piece of work. You know that?" he said.

"Yes, sir. I'm not allowed to be argumentative, so you must be correct."

"Well, I called to see if you two were okay. I got my answer, so now I can hang up."

"Don't you dare. How is everything going for you?"

He spent the next ten minutes telling her about Salas' revelation. Now she understood why she was allowed to bring Joshua to work. It wasn't just a precaution it was a necessity. She wasn't at all pleased that he hadn't told her right away.

"Is anything else happening? I've been so busy with this Penelope crap that I have neglected all my other duties."

"That's probably why so many people call up to tell me you're a jerk. That and not telling your fiancee she's still in danger."

"Ellie, I just told you. What do you want?"

"Jeremy, you should have called me last night. It could have been important."

"Honey, it was too late. The only thing I would have accomplished is to rob you of a good night's sleep. Just keep your eyes open now. I'll be there in a bit."

"We'll be here. Love you and be careful."

"You too." The conversation was over.

They were two people stuck in a situation that defied explanation for anyone not living the nightmare along with them. Cain was at a loss as to how to continue handling his normal day to day duties while a murderous entity stalked all those that had wronged it, including those trying to stop it now.

In his own mind he likened the experience to trying to play a sport, any sport, while someone was shooting at you. Your concentration was out the window and your next breath could be your last. The pressure was getting to him.

He prayed Carl and Tom could come up with something. He understood their reluctance. They were wounded, but still in danger. He personally was way too far out of his element. He gathered his thoughts and tried to calm himself down. Once he accomplished that, he headed for the office. He couldn't let Ellie and Joshua see how scared he was.

After a ten minute drive, he pulled into the park office parking lot. He got out of his SUV, bounded up the steps and entered with a big smile. "Hey troops. What's happening in the parks today?"

"Booger called. You're supposed to call him back," Ellie informed him.

"Since when did you start calling Tom, Booger?"

"I don't know. Seemed appropriate I guess. He snorted twice while I was on the phone with him. He has serious nasal issues," she commented.

"I accidentally called him Booger the other day. I lied and told him it was a childhood thing and that I called everyone Booger."

"Who's Booger?" Joshua asked as he emerged from the back room.

"He's one of Jeremy's playmates, sweetie."

"Wow. You have a friend named Booger. I know a kid named Booger too, but you wouldn't want to be friends with him. He's always picking his nose and wiping his boogies on people," Joshua said with the offended sincerity of a child.

Ellie and Cain stifled the giggles that wanted to bubble up. Joshua had no clue as to the humor being generated by this conversation. He just knew he didn't want a friend named Booger.

Cain and Ellie both jumped when the phone rang. Stealing moments of normalcy caused both of them to forget the dire situation that still lay ahead and presumably unresolved.

Ellie answered the phone and passed it to Cain. It was Booger himself.

"What's up, Tom?"

"Warden Cain, we think we have an idea. A good idea," Tom assured.

"Tell me about it," Cain requested.

"No. We want to meet you here on campus. Come to the Earth Science Building. Room 1210 at noon. Then we will reveal our plan. Okay?"

"I'll be there," Cain assured and hung up.

It was already ten-thirty. The drive to State College was almost an hour, so Cain said his goodbyes to his future family and hit the road.

At eleven forty-seven Cain found himself standing in room 1210. He was early, but a pretty lab assistant was showing him some of the rock and mineral specimens that the Geology Department was particularly proud of.

He didn't want to be rude, so he feigned interest. The young woman was very into these rocks. *This pretty girl should be excited about many things, but rocks shouldn't be one of them,* he thought.

Carl entered the room, but wasn't his usual smiley self. He sported bandages on his jaw and the left side of his scalp. Booger followed close behind. Cain smiled mentally at Joshua's earlier reaction to Booger. He too was bandaged, but only on his right forearm.

"Good afternoon, Warden Cain, since it is now two minutes after the noon hour," Carl said rather petulantly.

"Hey, Jeremy," Booger said with the hint of a smile. Apparently Carl was taking the lead on setting the tone for the meeting, but Cain noticed Tom's more friendly, familiar greeting.

"Gentlemen," Cain replied, waiting to see where this was headed.

"I'm not happy that you are drawing us back into this, Cain. I'll be blunt. I do not want to be anywhere near the action sequence of this plan. Understood?" Carl asserted.

"Got it," Cain answered. He was keeping his answers brief. He could feel himself bristling at Carl's tone.

"Tom, you explain it to him," Carl ordered.

"No problem," Booger said. "It's like this, Jeremy. We took an additional step to research the assertions about Penelope being a witch. We found two journals that mention her by name in the archives of the Blair County Historical Society. Both are in agreement that the woman was into the black arts.

"We then looked for any corroboration that witches could control wild beasts and dumb animals. The connection was there all along. We just missed it because it had been dumbed down over the centuries."

"Meaning what? She's now back to being a witch for real?" Cain asked.

"Jeremy, did you ever hear the term *familiar* in regards to witches?"

"Yeah, sure. Witches had a familiar, most often black cats as helpers or something like that. Right?"

Booger grinned broadly. "Very good, but that's kind of the child's version of the story. The broader story is that they employed many different types of animals for different purposes.

"Dark colored cats were used for a specific purpose. Spying. They were naturals at doing a witch's bidding at night because of their color and stealth.

"Wolves were used as assassins, which explained the long held belief of the existence of werewolves and lycanthrope. Birds of various kinds were used as messengers, spies and collectors of rare ingredients for witches' potions.

"Bears were used to intimidate. Rats to spread sickness and disease, usually as revenge for some slight to the witch. And retarded, or mentally challenged, humans were used for a plethora of duties. The witch can work her magic on simple minds.

"Interesting side note, domesticated dogs were unattainable subjects. Canine loyalty to their humans, and humankind in general, kept them off the servant's list of witches. Dogs really are man's best friend."

"Okay, so now I can feel good about buying a dog. What does all this prove?" Cain inquired rather testily. Carl's silent body language was getting to him. The man kept tapping his fingers and rolling his eyes as if he had somewhere, so much more important, to be.

"Well, we believe that it may prove that Penelope is not just a pissed off ghost, but is in fact a pissed off dead witch. The importance of that is that now we don't move forward to put a simple spirit to rest, but rather we act to kill a witch a second and final time. Whole different ball game."

"Good God! Are you two done with the child's lesson on who the hell she was? Get to the plan!" Carl screamed.

Cain had had enough. "You listen to me, you impatient asshole. Rita and Father Mulcahey are dead! They didn't die in the woods. They died in their homes. And in case you need a child's explanation, Professor, she is still out there and she isn't done killing! We all may still be on her short list. Maybe there's a fricking cat listening to this conversation right now. If so, you better get back on-board with the rest of us or take your chances on your own!" Cain finished and saw movement out of the corner of his eye.

He turned to find the pretty lab assistant staring directly at him and looking scared or mortified. Maybe both. He had forgotten that she was still in the room.

"Veronica," Booger said looking at the poor woman. "We are part of a drama group. This is part of the exercises we do to stay sharp. You can leave now. You don't need to hear any more of our foolishness."

Booger knew it was a lame cover story, but he was out of his element. He never saw her when he entered the room. He wished he had.

She left immediately.

"Holy shit. This is going to get out and make us sound like a bunch of kooks," Carl moaned.

Cain helped him put things in perspective. "I hate to tell you guys this, but you already are considered to be a bit on the eccentric side by faculty and students alike. At least that's what Rita had told me."

"She's gone. So here's the plan," Booger continued. "There are two naturally occurring substances that witches hate. Any guess as to what they are?"

"Holy shit, Tom. Just tell him," Carl spat out continuing with his impatient routine.

Cain ignored him. "Fire and brimstone?"

"No, but not a bad guess. Salt and amber. Amber and salt," Booger said with a bit of glee in his voice.

Cain bit, if not to make Booger happy, then to prolong Carl's misery. "Why those two? Oh, and must they be used together?"

"No, they need not be used together, but why not? If one is going for the kill, so to speak. Amber is a substance that once lived and predates man's existence, therefore predates any control man may have over it. It interacts with light in beautiful ways and witches hate it. Unfortunately, we don't have a more specific reason.

"And salt, because it is caustic and naturally occurring. Witches, once becoming a proper witch that is, cannot cross saltwater. So Penelope became a witch once she arrived here."

"But who taught her?" Cain asked.

"Most likely a book sent along with her from Europe. European witches did that shit. Kind of like witch evangelism. Spreading their misery to the New World through innocent young women who would turn dark by the use of their witch training manuals.

"Or, less likely, an Indian shaman or medicine man. Or a tribal oracle. They were usually women," explained Booger.

"They were associated with lycanthropy at times and close association with the owl. It was their favorite familiar and was sent out as a warning and sometimes a spy. Crazy stuff, I know."

"So what's the plan?" asked Cain.

"Hot damn. Finally," interjected Carl, still being an asshole in Cain's opinion.

It wasn't lost on Cain that Carl was acting the way he was because he was scared to death. But the truth was that they all were.

"Here's the deal, Jeremy. We need to find her bones again and reduce them to ashes mixed with amber and salt. No matter what, her current animated spiritual force is tied to her bones. They were her earthly connection when she was alive. When they cease to exist, she ceases to exist," Booger explained.

"So why the amber and salt?" asked Cain.

Tom smiled at Jeremy. "We don't know how strong she really is. If she can keep the ashes of her bones together, then her bones still exist. The salt and amber will break any cohesive bond. The elements will cause chaos and dissolution. We can then scatter the ashes far and away and she's done."

"And how do we know all this?" Cain inquired.

"Do you really want to know?" asked Carl.

"Yes. We already thought she was done once. And maybe she is. Since Salas' revelation she hasn't done shit. So maybe he was wrong," Cain pointed out.

"No, he was right. I had the same impression that day, but I thought I was being paranoid," Booger responded.

"Me too," Carl added, "but we were up to our assholes in alligators, so I never got a chance to key in on it."

"Those were snakes and coyotes, Carl. Not alligators," Cain corrected, hoping to add a note of levity.

They didn't laugh, but a shared smile broke a little of the tension.

"So to answer your question, Jeremy, we asked a local coven of witches to help us with our dilemma. They are white witches. Good guys, so to speak."

Cain moaned and leaned back against a display table full of rocks. "Guys, my belief systems have taken a serious hit this year. Bigfoot, ghosts and witches weren't even on my radar over a month ago. Now my whole life hangs in the balance based upon my believing in them all. Not fair. Not fair at all."

Carl had softened his demeanor quite a bit. "Warden Cain, we were there too. We had connections and experiences, but all this crap wasn't much more than a hobby for us old eccentrics. We dabbled in this shit because it was exciting to think about the *what if* of it all.

"But now it has all become a reality crashing down around our ears. Dead colleagues and attacks on our own lives was never part of the game. Well, it is now and we're scared as hell."

"Salt we can buy by the bag. Where do we get the amber?" Cain asked.

"Actually, it has to be naturally occurring salt. Nothing processed and as for the amber, you're standing next to it. That yellow blob behind you is petrified tree sap. We need to steal it when we walk out of here. That's why I wore my cargo shorts. Hand it here. I'll stick it in one of my big pockets and we can leave.

"Oh, there's one other thing that needs to be mixed with her ashes," Booger said rather sheepishly.

"Oh brother. What?" Cain demanded.

"The ashes of an Asio Otis," Booger replied.

"What? A long-eared owl! They're endangered. We can't. I'm sworn to protect endangered creatures," Cain exclaimed.

Carl looked at Cain and said matter-of-factly, "it's them or us, Warden Cain. Would you choose an owl over another human life?"

"Let's get going. If I have to sell my soul, I want to get it over with," Cain said angrily. He turned and picked up a translucent yellow lump of petrified tree sap and handed it to Booger. He then walked out disgusted at what this endeavor would require of them all before it was over.

Chapter 29

Giving A Hoot

Cain spent the previous evening explaining the next plan to Salas, Doreemer and Ellie. They met again the next morning, minus Ellie, at Warden Smith's memorial service. It was a bad day.

After the service, Cain went over to Smith's widow to express his condolences. He should have been in contact with her before this, but nothing was as it should be.

Maddie Smith looked at Cain with unconcealed anger. The slap that struck Cain's face came so quickly that he didn't even flinch.

"Your men are dropping like flies. What are you doing about it? Do you even care? Or are you too busy with your new fiancee to really give a shit? How could you let my husband be torn apart by coyotes while you stood by?"

Cain was stunned, first by the slap and secondly by the intensity of her anger. He was nauseated by her accusations, but could not come up with a defense in the wake of her sorrow.

Everyone in attendance looked on as Jeremy hung his head in hurt and shame. He knew there was some truth to her words. His men were dying and he was helpless to stop it. Warden Smith had been on the firing line because he had put him there. He was doing the same to Salas and Doreemer, and Ellie for that matter.

He stepped back and whispered, "I'm sorry, Maddie." Then he turned and walked slowly to the parking lot with his head hung low. He felt defeated.

"It's not your fault, Jeremy." It was Booger. He and Carl had been in attendance. "She had no right to say that."

"Tom, she had every right. She just lost her husband and I was so busy with our witch hunt that I didn't even go see her. I dropped the ball and she feels abandoned and betrayed. She's pretty damn right about it all."

Ellie couldn't be at the service because of a scheduled doctor's appointment for Joshua. He was glad. She shouldn't see him like this, he thought, especially since Maddie accused him of dereliction because of his relationship with her.

Salas came up with Doreemer and said, "Jeremy, she was out of line."

Several other Wardens were in attendance. They were clustered together by the front of the hearse that would carry Smith's body to his plot at the cemetery. All eyes were on Cain.

"No, Warden Salas. She has it pretty much straight. At least from her perspective. Now if you'll excuse me, I have a date with an Asio Otis."

He walked away and got into his car. One hundred sets of eyes were on him as he pulled out of the parking lot. He was on a mission.

Next stop, Blair County Wildlife Rescue Center.

Forty-five minutes later he was at his next stop.

"Yes, Warden Cain, we have two owls almost ready to be returned to the wild. Why the sudden interest?" Rebecca Martin asked. She was the Center's Director and one of two full-time employees. All the others there were volunteers.

"What can I say? I love owls and my fiancee's little boy loves owls. He wants to help rescue them. I thought releasing one back into the wild would be a good start."

"What's his name?" Rebecca asked.

"Who?"

"Your fiancee's little boy."

"Oh, his name is Joshua. Cute as a button. So can I take one of the owls?"

"Warden Cain, this is highly unusual. Releasing a bird back into its habitat is not just a matter of letting it fly away or setting it on a branch and waving goodbye."

"Okay. Teach me."

"Come back later this afternoon and I'll give you a crash course. Are you sure about this?"

"Yes. I want to learn to do it right," he lied.

Three hours later he returned. Rebecca was ready.

"I made some calls about you. You enjoy a sterling reputation in Harrisburg. They told me to cooperate if I could. So let's get started. That's a raptor box," she said pointing at a fibre board box with a round hole and a dowel rod sticking out of it.

"Okay. A raptor box," he repeated, sounding and feeling slightly idiotic.

You must attach this to a tree, about fifteen feet off the ground. This has been Ozzie's home and will be his home in the wild until he decides otherwise," she instructed.

"Oh shit, don't give it a damn name. Ozzie sounds too warm and fuzzy," he thought to himself.

"Ozzie will adjust just fine. You should check on him every day if possible. He hunts for himself, so he'll do well. Greta hasn't caught onto hunting yet, so we'll keep her for a few more weeks," she informed him.

He didn't care about Greta. He just needed Ozzie. *Just give me the damn bird, lady,* he impatiently played in his head over and over again, like a broken record.

Before long he had the raptor box covered by a blanket. The owl was inside. Ozzie was inside. He chuckled. He was working with an Ozzy Osbourne look-alike and now he had an owl named Ozzie. He wondered if the bird picked his beak in front of the other birds….Booger the Owl.

The last thing he remembered hearing was Rebecca saying, "I hope Joshua enjoys the experience." To which he replied, "thanks a million." And then drove away as fast as he possibly could without raising suspicion.

He thought to himself, *a bird in hand is better than two in the bush.* He had grown up hearing that old axiom all the time. Now he knew it was true. He had their coveted bird.

The biggest problem in his immediate future was helping to destroy an animal that he was sworn to protect. He hated the choice he had to make, but it was clear. Saving human lives always trumped saving an animal. Ozzie the Owl was toast.

Chapter 30

She's Back

The next day, Cain spent the morning on a conference call with Harrisburg. The Director of the State Parks Systems was a man fairly high up in the Pennsylvania Department of Conservation and Natural Resources. His name was Alfred Moynihan and he was concerned about the Western District in general.

Moynihan and several of his *yes men* were grilling Cain about recent events. Death was a very unpopular subject inside the boundaries of the State forests. The Bigfoot phenomenon was still in full swing as well.

That last fact was eating away at Moynihan. With the Bigfoot notoriety, he thought the parks should be full of people hoping to catch a glimpse. But the unhappy truth is that the Pennsylvania Bigfoot had proven to be a sociopath.

That is, assuming one considers Bigfoot a human, Cain thought to himself. Moynihan really was a piece of work.

Moynihan readily admitted that the recent events and multiple deaths were beyond Cain's control, but the perception was that they happened on his watch. The concern was that park attendance in the Western District had fallen off sharply, with the exception of the Bigfoot hunters. People perceived the parks were unsafe. Budget time was closing in and monies had to be justified by public attendance.

Beyond his mild scolding, Cain felt that he actually made some headway. Harrisburg promised him seven more officers. He couldn't wait. The first three would be replacements for their recent losses, but the additional four would be a step in the right direction to bolster his meager force.

Moynihan and his cronies likened the additional wardens with putting more cops on the street. They had no idea the vastness of the western wilderness areas, but Cain wasn't going to open his mouth. He needed the additional manpower.

After the conference call, he immediately called Booger and Carl to discuss the steps needed to finish this whole unpleasant business. He couldn't wait to hand over Ozzie to Booger. His guilt mechanism was working overtime.

Ozzie was sharing his home, for lack of anywhere else to keep him. He was not a good houseguest. Noise and stink were the sum total of the bird's contributions to the roommate situation.

Early in the afternoon, around twelve forty-five, the phone rang. Ellie answered and Cain watched her stiffen and turn white as a ghost as she pivoted to tell him to take line two. He knew this wasn't going to be good.

It was Doreemer. "Sir, we have a situation in Rothrock above the State College area."

"Doreemer, I don't know what *a situation* means and I'm all out of patience and decorum. Cut the crap and detail what it is."

"Yes, sir. Multiple deaths. Four locals from the Tyrone area were out hunting Bigfoot. There was more beer than ammo present at their campsite. The victims appeared to have been attacked by a pack of raccoons. Really big ones," Doreemer supplied.

Cain couldn't help correcting her. "A group of raccoons are called a *gaze*. And how do you know they were big?"

"Three of them are dead, along with our victims. I already weighed one and it was over twenty-five pounds. The other two are approximately the same size. From the tracks that we have found, we have determined there were at least fifteen to twenty."

"Wait a minute," Cain halted her, "raccoons around here usually top out at twenty pounds. And their social groups never exceed six or seven individuals. Are you sure about your estimate?"

"It is just an estimate, Warden Cain, but I believe that my estimate could even be on the low side. And as far as the size, I'm being accurate. These suckers are huge. I wouldn't want to face-off with one of them, let alone a whole herd. Whoops, sorry. A whole *gaze*."

"I'll be there in about an hour. Is Salas there?" Cain asked.

"No, sir. He's on his way. Should be here in about thirty."

"Don't move too much around over there. I have to see this myself. Do you have a good camera?" he asked.

"Yessir. I have the point and shoot from the State. Ten megapixel. It does pretty well."

"Okay, see you in a bit." Cain then hung up, said goodbye to Ellie and headed out.

On the drive to investigate the latest murders, because that was how Cain thought of them, Booger called. Cain told him where he kept his spare key under a flowerpot along the side of the house. He told Booger to get

Ozzie out of his house as soon as possible. Booger promised that when Cain got home, Ozzie the Owl would be long gone and that suited Cain to a T.

Cain entered the park at access point fourteen. He knew where Doreemer was. She had told him she was within rock throwing distance of trailhead twenty-one. It was a popular trail in the winter. Many hunters used it during deer season which was fast approaching.

By the time he pulled up, Salas had arrived along with the medical examiner, a State Policeman and an EMT crew. They were always sent in case a live victim was found. That wasn't the case here. Doreemer had verified that this party was only four strong.

She had run into another Bigfoot group who had contact with the group of deceased men. They confirmed it was a quartet. They had a lot of questions, but Doreemer shut them down and moved them on.

Cain's first reaction to the scene was that something extremely chaotic had occurred. He tried counting the number of attackers and agreed with Doreemer that her earlier estimate may have been on the light side.

This was crazy, which meant Penelope was at work once again. It wasn't lost on Cain that everyone here at the site might be in danger. If the masked marauders took on four heavily armed men, then this group were sitting ducks.

Only Doreemer, Salas, the State Policeman and himself were armed and only with pistols. The coroner and ambulance crew would be helpless.

Cain pulled Doreemer and Salas aside and shared his concern. They both understood and returned to their vehicles to get their shotguns. The State Police officer expressed his curiosity as to why the Wardens grabbed their extra artillery.

Cain didn't pull any punches. "The raccoons may be diseased and still in the area. This kind of attack would certainly indicate that."

The State Officer walked quickly over to his patrol car and got his own shotgun. Cain had never seen anyone looking so nervous.

The next step Warden Cain took was to ask the coroner to expedite the proceedings. The Wardens continued to look for any additional clues, but knowing who was behind this made their efforts more for show for the others present than anything else.

When the fourth and final body was loaded into the coroner's wagon, Cain breathed a sigh of relief. It was relief for everyone's safety, but much more. He now could empty Rothrock, claiming diseased raccoons were on the loose and had attacked humans. He wanted the Bigfoot hunters and everyone else out of harm's way until Penelope was shut down for good.

He also knew Moynihan and his boys weren't going to like it. He was now going to change the perception of the forests being unsafe to a certainty. Most people would translate his *diseased* description into *rabid*. He didn't care as long as it kept them away.

He would leave here and begin the process that would most likely cause his eventual firing. He couldn't worry about that. Lives were on the line. He could launch a campaign to save himself later.

Warden Jeremy Cain was near his breaking point. The deaths of strangers and friends were weighing heavily upon his heart. The discovery of the existence of Bigfoot and a ghostly, evil witch at the center of it all, had him on edge as well. But that wasn't the worst of it.

He now found himself engaged to a woman that he had only known three months. And she had a kid to boot. In the midst of the most emotionally charged chaotic period of his career he somehow decided to end his hard earned bachelorhood.

He had been through several long-term girlfriends, but never had he thought about getting married. He worked long hours and needed his freedom to do his job well.

He found himself driving back to the office and saying aloud, "what in the hell was I thinking? I could be torn apart by giant raccoons or slapped silly by a colony of beaver with big tails. She must have been crazy to say yes. It's too late now. I am a man of my word. I'm committed or I should be committed. One or the other."

His drive continued to be an animated soliloquy all the way back. When he pulled into the parking lot, he noticed the office lights were on and Ellie's car was still present. It was hours after closing time.

He walked in the front door of the park Welcome Center
& Warden's Office and was assailed, first by the smell of roasted chicken, secondly by the aroma of cinnamon rolls, and thirdly by a hug and a kiss from his fiancee.

He felt a vise-like grip on his leg and looked down. Joshua was giving him a big hug too. In that moment he knew with certainty that this was exactly what he wanted.

Now he just needed to stay alive long enough to enjoy it.

Chapter 31

Last Ditch Effort

Snow. It was sometimes seen before Halloween, but not this year. Flurries yes, but no accumulation had occurred. This was the first week of December and the snow was falling lightly. The forecast was for one to two inches.

To people in these parts it was a dusting, not even cause for concern. To Jeremy and his cohorts it was a slight nuisance. They needed to retrieve Penelope's bones.

Everyone thought finding the original spot was going to be a problem. It wasn't. Unbeknownst to everyone else, Booger had anticipated that the need to keep tabs on the witch's grave may be necessary. He had taken it upon himself to slip a disc of iron under the bones when they had laid them out for burial last time.

Being the owner of a metal detector made Booger, currently, the team's most valuable player. The team stood together in the clearing next to the creek.

A week and a half had passed since the raccoon attack. Penelope had fallen silent, which was a good thing. Jeremy couldn't take much more. Harrisburg had been breathing down his neck and talk of his removal had been threatened.

Ellie had tried hard to create some normalcy by making Thanksgiving dinner for the three of them. She did a great job, but lately all food was tasteless to Jeremy. Stress and grief had robbed him of even the smallest of pleasures. He was listless when playing with Joshua. Even their lovemaking was put on hold.

He was withdrawing from Ellie slowly because he didn't want to drag her and Joshua down with him. Ellie refused to let him get away with it. She redoubled her efforts to be his support system. Whether Jeremy knew it or not, she was keeping him sane and grounded.

Ellie wasn't with them at the moment. Warden Cain had refused to allow her any closer to the danger than she already was. He asserted his authority to keep her safe. She understood.

The group, consisting of Cain, Salas, Doreemer, Carl, Booger and the grad student named James, surveyed the small white field in front of them.

James was a surprise to Cain. His arm was still heavily bandaged from his coyote bite as he stood holding his shovel. The kid had balls for sure.

Salsa spoke up while pointing. "Tom, start sweeping dead center between that maple and the creek embankment."

"Yeah, that's the way I remember it too. Almost dead center between the tree and the water," Booger replied.

He began a methodical sweep with his metal detector. In the first five minutes they got a hit. James began to dig. What they found was an old, rusted pocketknife. A Boy Scout logo could still be discerned on the bolster of the blade end.

Booger resumed his search. Another hit only three minutes later. James repeated his digging routine. Another false alarm. This time they unearthed a large assembled and rusted bolt, washer and nut. The size of it had them all agreeing it was a part off of a piece of farm equipment.

Without a word, Booger began to once again sweep the area. Ten minutes went by. He was moving very slowly. A loud pinging sound emanated from his rig. James began his routine, a little more slowly this time. His fourth spade of dirt revealed two rib bones. Pay Dirt!

Doreemer joined in with her shovel. Within thirty minutes every bone was accounted for according to Carl. The plan was now to remove the bones and take them to a local incinerator that was owned by a local demolition company. The owner was a friend of Cain's.

It wasn't lost on Cain that they had not been confronted by snakes, coyotes, bears or mountain lions. *Yet,* he thought to himself.

The bones were boxed up and the group began the trek back to their vehicles. Everyone was on high alert. Nerves were stretched taut and were raw. Each of the persons in their party expected an attack.

They moved faster with each step closer towards their escape. No one spoke. They needed to be able to hear any possible sign of encroaching hostile animals. None came.

They drove away in Cain's SUV and Carl's Honda Civic. Carl followed Cain to his friend's business address. The incinerator had been thoroughly cleaned and was fired up and waiting.

It was an expensive venture to power an incinerator and Cain's friend had done it, no questions asked. That was the kind of respect Cain had cultivated among his friends and acquaintances.

The only thing the friend made Cain do was to promise to tell the whole story when it was done, over a steak dinner. Cain's treat, of course.

Upon their arrival, the team wasted no time entering the metal structure that held the large oven. Carl held the box of bones and all but broke into a run when he saw the door to the incinerator. But before he got too close, he halted along with everyone else.

They could only stare in disbelief. A figure had walked out of the shadows. It was Warden Smith. He stood angrily glaring at them. He was in uniform. A bloody uniform. His throat was a wet, gaping hole. He was trying to speak.

The incinerator was relatively quiet, considering its size, but it still put out a dull roar. Smith's words were garbled and wet sounding and were eaten up by the sound of the fire in the huge furnace.

Salas was the one to break the silence. "Jeremy, what the hell do we do now?"

Carl followed up with, "this is bullshit!"

James had brought along the shovel. Cain grabbed it and walked towards Smith.

He raised the spade like a batter ready to swing and then did exactly that. The blade of the shovel passed through the apparition of Smith. Smith became a large puff of gray smoke.

Cain turned to Carl and said, "you're right, Carl. It was bullshit. Now let's get this done." He then turned to Doreemer and told her to go back and make sure the door was shut behind them. He figured they didn't need to fight with any animals that may sneak up on them.

Cain's friend was nowhere to be seen. They moved ahead without him. Booger began to set up a little work table on a nearby flat topped cart. He had assembled sea salt, pulverized amber, the ashes of good old Ozzie the Owl and needed only Penelope's ashes to complete the recipe for exterminating the witch.

Carl set the bone box down. He grabbed an iron bar that was obviously used to open and shut the small door they would use for this cremation. Carl bent to the task. The door suddenly flew open with force and a stream of living fire engulfed Carl.

At first the remaining five were stunned. The fire was definitely acting unnaturally. It appeared to lunge and almost embrace Carl. His screams broke their paralysis.

James saw a wall fire extinguisher and employed it to put out the fire on Carl. Cain had run forward and picked up the bar and shut the furnace door. But it was too late for Carl. James had extinguished the flames quickly, but their friend was already dead.

Cain looked at Booger and yelled, "what the hell was that?"

"Witches can sometimes control fire. She must be making a last ditch effort to stop us," Booger replied.

Doreemer yelled, "last ditch effort? Bullshit, Tom! That was a major coup if you ask me. Who the hell wants to reopen that door now?"

She was right. If Penelope could control the fire like that, then the incinerator idea was done.

Cain went over to Carl's body and picked up the box of bones the professor had dropped. He then looked at Booger.

"Come on, Tom. Think. How can we beat this bitch? There has to be a way."

"Look, on the wall," Booger said as he pointed to Cain's left. Hanging from a peg on the wall was a two-piece flame retardant safety suit. It was silver colored. One part was a jump style suit and the second part was a hood that covered the shoulders and head. It had a rectangular glass faceplate.

Salas went to the suit and discovered heavy silver gloves stuffed in a pouch hanging from the front of the suit. It was a complete fire safety suit. It even had footies to cover the wearer's shoes. This was their answer.

James said, "wish we would have seen this before the professor opened that door."

Cain had almost forgotten that James was just a kid and had now witnessed his teacher and mentor burned to death. He wondered if this young man would need therapy after this was all over. Maybe they all would.

Salas began donning the fire suit.

"Mitch, let me put that on," Cain insisted.

"No, sir. My turn to do something," he answered.

Doreemer said out loud to no one in particular, "do you think Smith was here to stop us or warn us?"

Booger spoke up, "I don't think that was Smith at all. It was one of Penelope's tricks. That's all."

A minute or two of silence passed between them until Salas affirmed he was ready.

He stood in front of the door holding the bar that would open the furnace door in one hand. In the other hand he was holding the box of bones. If Penelope directs a stream of fire his way, he will hold the box front and center. Let her incinerate herself.

The others moved back. Cain held the extinguisher in case it was needed again. They watched Salas slowly open the furnace door.

Flames shot out as before, but this time the intended victim was protected by the fire suit. Salas held up the box as a shield and the flames enveloped the container for a second and then receded. Penelope knew she was causing her own destruction.

The flames pulled back behind the furnace door and then the furnace went dark. The witch extinguished the fire. Within moments they heard the ticking and pings of cooling metal.

Salas didn't take any chances. He closed and locked the furnace door before he removed his hood.

"Now what do we do?" he asked the group.

Cain was pissed. He couldn't quite explain why, but being outsmarted by a dead witch was certainly at the center of the problem.

He walked across the room to an acetylene rig that was used for repairs on the furnace. He turned to the witch fighters and said, "if we can't do it the easy way, then we'll do it the hard way."

He put on a pair of goggles that were hanging off one of the tanks, found the friction lighter and asked Salas to bring him the box of bones.

He opened the box and began to torch each individual bone. It would take a while, but this had to end today.

That's when several rats made an appearance.

Doreemer screamed, "look at the floor drain!"

Rats were slowly popping up and into the room. The drain cover was off and laying to its side.

James began swinging his shovel at the rats while making his way to the drain. The rats were giving him a wide berth. They weren't near as ferocious as the other animals Penelope had controlled.

He kicked the drain cover into place and stood on it. The rats attacked and he deflected several with the shovel blade. Salas had joined him and was dispatching several with the furnace door bar.

Doreemer was using her shotgun to blast a group here and there. Cain ignored them all. He was single-minded of purpose. Several of the smaller bones were already charred black and ready to be crushed to ashes. He hoped the tanks held enough fuel to finish the job.

Cain screamed, "OUCH! A little help over here!" A rat had bitten Cain's ankle, twice. The pain was excruciating, but he continued torching the bones.

Salas ran over to Cain and flattened the rat that had bitten him. He then stood guard over Cain while James, Doreemer and Booger ran after the remaining rats.

If they survived this, Salas promised himself a good laugh. He was watching Tom chasing the rats with a hammer. Each time he swung, he covered his face with his handkerchief that he had pulled from his pocket. It was marked and dotted with gore. The hammer blows that hit the mark produced blow-back from the squashed rats.

Normally rats couldn't be targeted so easily, but these rats were sluggish. Maybe their little brains were having difficulty following orders and processing Penelope's rage all at once.

Ten minutes after the rat attack started, it was over. Doreemer had squashed some with the butt of her shotgun.

James killed all within reach of the drain. He never stopped standing on it. He could still see rats through the grate.

"Hey guys, find me something to hold this drain cover down," James begged.

Booger pushed a flat cart filled with wood scraps over to James and positioned a wheel to hold the cover down. James relaxed and walked away from the drain.

Doreemer and Booger were bite-free, but James had three bites, Salas two and Cain two. They shared their concerns about the diseases the rats might be carrying.

Cain ignored them and soldiered on. He was becoming exhausted. Salas offered to take over, but Jeremy acted as if he hadn't heard him. His dedication was in part due to his desire for Ellie, Joshua and himself to have a normal life. A boring life with no witches, mythical beasts or wild animals trying to kill them. That thought was interrupted.

A shriek pierced the relative quiet of the room. A few moments had passed with only the steady, low air-flow noise of the torch. It made the shriek seem like it filled the whole building.

It was unnerving and angry sounding and something else. It sounded wounded and pitiable, although no pity would come Penelope's way from this group.

"Look!" Doreemer yelled.

All eyes, even Cain's, were focused on the far end of the building near the door they had entered.

A woman in a white gown stood facing them. Her straggly hair hung down and covered her face. She was breathing heavily, which hit Cain as odd. He thought a *dead* witch would have no reason to breath at all.

She stiffened, hands rigid at her sides, and shrieked again.

"Doreemer, what's wrong?" Salas yelled.

Jane Doreemer was swaying back and forth. A large red spot was growing at the crotch of her pants. She collapsed.

Cain and Salas ran over to her. She appeared to be hemorrhaging.

"Jane! Jane! Can you hear me?" Cain said loudly.

Jane looked up at him and said, "the bitch just killed my baby! Don't ask me how I know, but I do. I haven't even told my husband yet. Stop her, Jeremy! End it!" She then passed out.

Jeremy let Salas take her. He stood and returned to the torch. "Tom, get your shit over here. We're going to start the process and send her to Hell!"

Booger ran to his cart and wheeled it over to Cain.

Cain handed him charred bones to pulverize and mix with the alabaster, salt and Ozzie the Owl.

Booger began the process and Penelope shrieked even louder, but this time there was no mistaking the pain in her cry. It was working.

This whole time James was staring in disbelief. This day was proving to be too much. His hands had turned white from gripping the shovel very tightly.

Salas noticed James had become a statue.

"James, are you okay?" Salas yelled.

"Depends on how you define *okay!*" he yelled back. "I think I peed myself during her last scream. What should I do?"

Before Salas could answer, Penelope moved forward very quickly. She covered thirty feet without moving her legs. It looked like a cheesy horror movie effect where the ghosts seemingly glide, but that is just what she did. She was only twenty feet away from James. He peed a second time.

Penelope's face was still masked by her hair. In the blink of an eye, she snapped her head up revealing soul-less black as ebony eyes. She looked right at James. His knees buckled and he went down as he passed out from the sheer terror of her appearance.

Salas understood James' reaction. He himself had to fight the urge to vomit. She was that revolting and scary. He was still sitting on the floor and holding Jane across his lap.

Doreemer was in and out of consciousness. She had stopped bleeding, but the trauma that Penelope had caused to her internally had taken a grave toll. She was pale and sweating profusely.

Cain continued to cremate the witch's body, bone by bone. He hadn't seen much of her since she appeared.

Booger was pulverizing and mixing the elements as quickly as Cain could supply him with more charred bone. The process was working.

The steady sound of the acetylene torch stopped abruptly. Cain quickly turned knobs and flicked the friction lighter over a dozen times. No more gas. No more fire. NO MORE HOPE.

Chapter 32

Turning The Heat Up

Booger dumped salt into his mixture. The powdered amber was almost used up, but the natural sea salt he had in great supply. As he churned his mixture, he thought of himself as a witch standing over her cauldron cooking up a witch's brew of misery.

He had amused himself with the thought even in the midst of this extreme terror. The salt became an inseparable and integral part of the ash and amber. Penelope shrieked once again, but the quality of terror it conveyed had diminished.

She was weakening. Her shriek sounded almost like a lament. It was working, but they needed more fire to finish the cremation of her skeleton. Cain finally turned to face her for the first time.

His blood turned to ice as she glared at him with dead, soul-less eyes. Again he noticed her breathing. Why this pretense of life from a spirit? Maybe it was just a memory of how to act in certain situations. He had heard long ago that ghosts that lingered hated being dead. They wanted to be alive again more than anything and did anything to keep that pretense alive.

"Tom, is everything mixed?" asked Booger.

"No, I still need the bones that you have left, and I haven't added the owl's ashes yet."

"Well, add the damn owl! She's already hurting. Maybe that will knock her down another peg."

Booger reached for Ozzie's ashes. They were gone. That's when he noticed a man standing about twenty feet away in the shadows. The man was holding the box with the owl's ashes.

"Cain, who the hell is that!" he said pointing at the new player in this drama. "He's got Ozzie's ashes!"

Cain spun around and followed Booger's outstretched arm and pointing finger. It was Kenneth Kottmeyer, the owner of this property and Cain's friend. Besides the fact that he was holding the ashes of the dearly departed owl, something was off. Cain knew it immediately.

"Ken, give us that box. Please! We need it!" Cain begged his friend.

Kottmeyer just stood staring, slack-jawed. His eyes appeared glazed over, as far as Cain could determine. His friend was acting strangely, to say the least. Of course, under these current circumstances, who had the right to say what was normal behavior.

"Ken, please hand me the box you are holding." Cain moved towards Kottmeyer. The man growled, or at least that was what it sounded like.

Penelope shrieked once more and Kottmeyer turned. He slowly and stiffly walked towards the furnace, maintaining an awkward gait.

"Oh, hell no!'' Cain said aloud. "Help me stop him, Tom. If he empties that into the furnace, we could lose the owl's ashes for good."

Both men converged on Kottmeyer. A shot rang out and Kottmeyer's head exploded. The man's body collapsed and the box of owl ashes fell to the floor.

Tom and Cain flinched and turned to see where the shot came from. Salas was standing fifteen feet behind them in a shooter's crouch.

"Why did you do that?" Cain shouted.

"We're losing Doreemer. This shit has got to stop! Grab the damn owl's ashes and mix them in. I spotted another tank of acetylene across the room. I'll get it. Get moving!"

Tom ran to the box of ashes, scooped it up and returned to his work station. He wasted no time mixing Ozzie's remains with the witch's ashes, powdered amber and sea salt.

Cain hadn't moved. He was still in shock at seeing his friend gunned down by one of his own men. He couldn't make sense of it. Salas had taken a hell of a step to end this.

Saving Doreemer was important, but at the cost of another life? This is not how this was to end. Too many had already died.

"He was already dead, Jeremy, or close to it. I just hastened the inevitable," Salas explained as he wheeled a spare acetylene tank over to where Cain had been working.

Cain looked at his subordinate and said, "explain yourself."

"Didn't you see how he was just standing there? He wasn't breathing. When he began walking, I knew."

"Knew what?" Cain yelled.

"Rigor mortis had set in. Didn't you see how he walked? He was stiff as a board. She was controlling him in some way. I just ended her connection. She had already killed him, probably before we got here.

"No more time to explain, Jeremy. Doreemer is slowly bleeding out. Turn the rest of those bones to ash and let's end this!"

"James, get over here!" Cain yelled. James had finally picked himself off the floor and had been observing the proceedings. This was almost too much for the young grad student to handle.

James moved quickly to Cain. "What can I do?"

"Keep charring these bones and feeding them to Tom." Cain paused and then turned to Salas. "Get her out. Take her to the hospital and don't come back. We'll either win or die trying. Go now! Save her!"

Salas hated to leave anyone behind, but James wasn't physically strong enough to handle Doreemer and Tom was needed here. Cain had a good handle on what needed to happen to finish the mission. Salas knew he was the only one who could save his bleeding partner.

Salas picked Doreemer up in a fireman's carry and moved towards the door they had entered, which seemed like hours ago. Cain stood guard over James and Tom.

Penelope yelled. The shriek was gone. Cain thought she somehow looked smaller. For the first time, she spoke.

"Stop! Stop! Please! You're killing me," she said.

"You're already dead," Cain responded. "You need to go to where dead people go. Leave! Get the hell out of here!"

"That's my only option. Hell, I never hurt anyone and they murdered me. On my wedding day they took me out in the woods and raped me. They took turns. Then they strangled me to death and buried me in the shallow grave where you found my bones."

Cain almost felt sorry for her. "If you're the victim, then why is Hell your only option?"

"I'm a witch. The first act a witch must take is to turn away from God. And I did. The first spell I cast was on the man I loved, but he didn't love me. I changed that. I stole his love.

"The women who exposed me were jealous. They hated me for wooing the most eligible man in the village. I should have silenced them, but my pride enjoyed their anger and pain too much. The only other men available were pathetic, toothless morons."

Her voice grew weaker as they spoke. Cain found it fascinating to be talking to this murderous ghost. She no longer seemed threatening.

Tom yelled, "almost done!"

James made his way over to stand beside Cain. "What's her excuse?" James asked.

"Shut up, boy. Why don't you go piss yourself again? Boo!"

She said this in a raspy whisper, but James still took a step back at the *boo*. Cain almost laughed.

"Done!" Booger yelled.

"Goodbye, Penelope." He then stepped forward holding the shovel James had held earlier. He swung it at her. She turned to vapor and disappeared. It was over. Finally.

Chapter 33

A New Normal

Explaining away the dead bodies of Carl and Kenneth Kottmeyer was rather difficult. The story that was manufactured by Cain, Salas, Doreemer, Booger and James was a doozy.

It made Ken into a deranged killer who attacked Carl with an incendiary device of some sort. Why they were even on the premises was just as difficult to explain, but since it involved three wardens, two professors and a grad student, it was accepted. They said they were planning on having Ken construct a Bigfoot trap out of steel. All the pieces and parts fit, except why Ken would go maniacal on them. Some of the State Police investigators felt they were being lied to, but there was not enough evidence to prove anything different.

It appeared Cain would keep his job. Salas too. Doreemer quit. She wanted to concentrate on making babies after her gynecologist gave her a clean bill of health.

Tom was heartbroken at having lost his best friend Carl. He began searching for teaching positions out West. James dropped out of school and began the pursuit of ghost hunting, along with several of his pot-smoking friends. He did have some real experience, but couldn't tell anyone because of their shared lie.

Ellie and Joshua were glad that Cain had more time for them. Ellie was especially glad that his job had just become extremely less dangerous with Penelope finally vanquished.

Christmas was almost upon all of them. It was made more sweet by having survived and successfully defeating a formidable opponent. Life was good.

She had traveled over seventy miles. For the last twenty-eight years they had sought each other out, their scents floating on the wind every late fall to early winter. It was their mating season. The desire was uncontrollable.

Monogamy among their kind was a lifelong venture. In twenty-eight years she had birthed seventeen live young. She raised them in solitary fashion.

Eleven month gestation and nine months of nurturing, then the offspring were forced for their own survival to live a solitary life. No social groups. A companion sought only during the rut.

Her companion was missing, although she could still smell stale whiffs of him every now and again. She continued her search.

Unbeknownst to her, she had entered the forest of Rothrock State Park. His scent was stronger here, but not fresh, like in years past. Her primitive brain registered alarm.

As she wandered, following his decaying olfactory signature, she found a definite trail to follow. And then she stood in a very small clearing, staring at a large shallow hole.

His presence had been strong here, but also the smell of the others. It was almost overwhelming.

The difference was that the others had left living scents. His was the smell of death. She knew her companion was no longer. As much as can be understood of her thought processes, she grieved. Her mate gone. The only explanation that she could piece together was that the others had killed him. She understood predator and prey relations.

She began to feel something. An emotion that was relatively foreign to her. Anger, tinged with hatred. The others had destroyed her mate. She would be childless this season.

The others were a threat. They had always avoided them. Now she knew why. They kill her kind.

The bubble of hatred began to grow. Her breathing had grown rapid and shallow. She had never felt this way before.

She heard a voice and her head snapped towards the sound. Them!

The three Bigfoot hunters walked lazily up the trail. They had been drinking most the afternoon, and looking at girlie magazines that the one had brought along.

They had no more interest in Bigfoot than the man on the moon. Getting away from their wives was their biggest reason for being out in the woods.

The fact is, they weren't even supposed to be here. Last thing they heard was the warnings about rabid raccoons. They figured it was all bullshit to scare away the Bigfoot enthusiasts. Screw'em. They would go where they wanted to go, when they wanted to go.

"Did you hear that?" asked the man wearing the Boston Red Sox baseball cap.

"Yeah. Sounded like somebody in pain or some thing," one of the companions added.

A crashing sound to their left had all three inebriated men spinning around to see what was happening.

A beast, bigger than they had ever seen, was charging right at them and covering ground faster than they could comprehend.

One man raised his shotgun and fired, removing the head of the man with the Red Sox cap. It was the only shot fired. The only shot that could be fired. The beast was too quick.

She attacked with a fury she had never felt before. The rage she felt had her acting instinctively. Her actions were no longer under her control, until the rage subsided. It felt wonderful.

Forty-five miles away the phone rang. Ellie picked it up. After less than a minute, Ellie turned to Jeremy. The look on her face made Jeremy's stomach do a flip.

"It's for you," she said softly. "It's not over."

.

Made in the USA
Monee, IL
09 July 2022

99346102R00154